International Praise for *Eurotrash*

"Christian Kracht's most intimate book, it is also a tender and cruel love letter to his ailing mother. The way Kracht ushers in this encounter [with his mother] and interweaves it with memories . . . is among the best things he has ever written; [*Eurotrash* is] chilling and heartbreaking."   —Jan Küveler, *Welt am Sonntag*

"This is the most touching, humanly mature novel Christian Kracht has written to date. And the funniest."
        —Denis Scheck, *SWR 2 lesenswert*

"*Eurotrash* creates so much pull and fascination that you simply can't tear yourself away from it. . . . This narrator offers more than its predecessor [*Faserland*], to which [he] refers. He is richer in experience, more aware of his mortality, more complex. This lends an unexpected, melancholy warmth to what is so far the best of Christian Kracht's magnificent novels."
        —Felix Müller, *Berliner Morgenpost*

"An astonishingly lighthearted story, a courageous novel that journeys into the heart of family horror without ever allowing itself to be crushed by it. It is unique among Christian Kracht's works and probably also in German-language literature."
        —Sebastian Hammelehle, *Der Spiegel*

"Kracht proves himself to be a sensitive writer with good humor and poignant insights. There are scenes in this book that blow you away—in part because you yourself often have the feeling that 'everything that does not rise into consciousness will return as fate.'"   —Ulrike Hug, *NZZ*

"Kracht's novel is a tremendous work about the destructive power of silence—over decades, over generations."
        —Volker Weidermann, *Spiegel Online*

EUROTRASH

ALSO BY CHRISTIAN KRACHT

The Dead

Imperium

EUROTRASH

· *A Novel* ·

CHRISTIAN KRACHT

Translated by Daniel Bowles

Liveright Publishing Corporation

A Division of W. W. Norton & Company
Independent Publishers Since 1923

First published in German by Verlag Kiepenheuer & Witsch in 2021.

This translation published with the support of the Swiss Arts Council Pro Helvetia.

For information about special discounts for bulk purchases, please contact W. W. Norton Special Sales at specialsales@wwnorton.com or 800-233-4830

Manufacturing by Sheridan
Book design by Lovedog Studio
Production manager: Anna Oler

ISBN 978-1-324-09456-2

Liveright Publishing Corporation, 500 Fifth Avenue, New York, N.Y. 10110
www.wwnorton.com

W. W. Norton & Company Ltd., 15 Carlisle Street, London W1D 3BS

1 2 3 4 5 6 7 8 9 0

*For my wife, my daughter,
my sister, and my mother.*

What is fully completely understood
leaves no trace as memory.

Jiddu Krishnamurti

. . . .

If you love Germany, you shouldn't visit it.

Jorge Luis Borges

EUROTRASH

I.

Anyway, so I had to go to Zurich again for a few days. My mother urgently wished to see me. On the phone she'd said I had better come quickly, please, which was so disturbing that I became terribly anxious and constipated the whole weekend long. Then there was this: I'd written a novel a quarter century ago called *Faserland*—a forgettable title—which ends in Zurich, out in the middle of the lake, somewhat traumatically.

The whole story came back to me again, in Zurich, down on Bahnhofstrasse, where I'd bought a dark brown, scratchy wool sweater at a sad little wooden stall, not far from Paradeplatz. It was already evening, and I'd taken some valerian, and the effect of the pills and the despair of an autumnal Switzerland and the twenty-five preceding years weighed, leaden beyond measure, on my mood.

Just before that I had been out in the Old Town. Over in Niederdorf there'd been an underground screening of *In girum imus nocte et consumimur igni*, the last film by Guy Debord, completed just before his suicide. Four or five people had come, which was a miracle on account of the still radiant evening warmth and that bloodless, soporific movie.

And after the audience, which is to say a pair of professors, the projectionist, and a homeless man who'd wanted to doze in the cinema seat for a while, had said their goodbyes and hands were shaken, I must have walked back down into the night toward Paradeplatz, without aim or purpose. And there, on the other side of the river Limmat, I came across a makeshift stall run by some Swiss commune, where two bespectacled women of indeterminate age and a kindly bearded young man were selling heavy wool sweaters and blankets in natural colors, which they had knitted themselves.

Compared to the clothing shown in the windows of the long closed but still brightly illuminated boutiques on Bahnhofstrasse, these simple woolen items possessed for me a homespun sort of authenticity, just as the women's smiles seemed, there's no other way to put it, suffused with reality and meaning. Certainly more real than the rest of Bahnhofstrasse, with its dozens upon dozens of Swiss flags hanging left and right, and the luxurious and useless baubles in the display cases. And, for a brief moment, when I passed them the hundred-franc bill, after taking off the sweater I'd impulsively tried on despite the chill, and receiving it, folded inside a light brown paper bag, I had the impression, perhaps also false, of having derived something meaningful from this transaction.

At any rate, I was handed the bag and a faded color brochure, which I accepted with mild embarrassment. I could dispose of it later unnoticed, I'd thought, and I said goodbye with an awkward smile and strolled toward Münsterplatz, shivering slightly, with the idea of having a drink at the bar of the Kronenhalle before returning to the hotel, climbing into bed, taking another herbal sleeping pill, and turning out the light.

I now understand that my mother's affairs, which had forced me to visit Zurich every other month, this city of poseurs and braggarts and debasements, had completely paralyzed me for years. The whole thing had become vile, altogether heinous, it had become more than I was able to bear, than one should normally have to bear. My mother was very sick, in the head, too—not just there, but primarily there.

In order not to lose her, and so as not to succumb to resignation and hopelessness, I'd decided at some point to visit her every other month. In fact, I'd simply decided to accept the misery in which my mother had been wasting away for decades in her apartment, surrounded by empty vodka bottles rolling about, unopened invoices from various Zurich sable-fur warehouses, and the crinkling foils of her packs of pain medication.

Now, though, she had contacted me of her own accord and summoned me to her; as a rule she had always just waited until I showed up, in that two-month rhythm, in Zurich. Usually she would ask me to tell her some stories. Her phone call made me, as I said, even more anxious than these visits already did because she must have had some ulterior motive.

She suddenly had the upper hand; she had taken the initiative, whereas she would otherwise always keep silent and wait.

She had neither email nor a mobile phone, and she spurned the internet. Too complicated, she would say, and the buttons were too small. I guessed, however, that she refused it all out of arrogance and not out of the simple inability to use a phone. She pretended to like reading the newspapers and Stendhal. Her skin had the texture of dry silk, and she was always slightly suntanned despite never sitting outside on the terrace, among the hydrangeas.

Her housekeeper stole from her. Every other day her wallet was empty. Although she almost never spent any money, it was all invariably gone, just as her black Mercedes was gone one day, too: taken from her apartment building's garage and transported off to Macedonia by the Macedonian husband of her Macedonian housekeeper. It was miserable, but at least she wasn't in Winterthur anymore.

For that was where she'd had to celebrate her eightieth birthday, on the closed psychiatric ward. If one were to have a sense of humor about it, the scene was like something out of Dürrenmatt, only it was much sadder than in Dürrenmatt because this was not just anyone's mother, but my mother, and not just any psychiatric ward, but the one bearing the darkest and cruelest name of all: Winterthur.

I had forgotten or repressed that the clinic had another name, something like *Frankenstein*. It was something along those lines, but I couldn't recall anymore. In any case, they'd released her from Winterthur—had been forced to release her, because only a court order could keep her in the mental hospital, and there wasn't one and there never would be one. You see, by her cunning manipulations, her brusque sangfroid, my mother knew how to convince whoever was examining her that everything was perfectly fine, that she had only to be allowed back into her apartment and everything would remain that way. She had only to be left to her phenobarbital, her cases of deplorable fendant—white wine in screw-top bottles at seven francs fifty—her subscription to the *Neue Zürcher Zeitung*, discontinued every week and promptly ordered again, and those mediocre expressionist paintings that her husband, my father, had given her during their marriage, while he'd of course kept the Noldes, Munchs, and Kirchners he'd filched in East Germany rolled up under his bed in the château on Lake Geneva, where he lived after divorcing her.

Thoughts of my late father's lost collection tormented me every time I learned that this or that work had been auctioned off at Grisebach in Berlin or at Christie's in London or at Kornfeld in Bern. They were pictures I had known since my earliest childhood, from our chalet in Gstaad. Every viscid brushstroke, every bluish yellow cloud trimmed in black, remained painfully familiar to me. And so, whenever I visited my mother, I was faced with the insolence of those third-rate German expressionist paintings hanging in her apartment, left over from our family's extraordinary collection. Pictures by Georg Tappert, for instance, or Max Kaus, and it's impossible to say what was more wretched: my mother's condition or those sorry daubs hanging on her walls in Zurich, like framed mockeries.

The disintegration of this family had a fathomless despair about it. And its low point was my mother's eightieth birthday in the common room of the Winterthur mental hospital. She had sat there, clutching her knees, her greasy ash blonde hair in a ponytail, wearing a pale blue terry cloth tracksuit. The eight-hundred-franc bouquet of flowers from Bahnhofstrasse on the table in front of her; the sunken palimpsest of her face bruised by a drunken fall and coated with deep red crusts of blood, her eyebrows barely discernible now, covered by the zigzag of lacerations stitched up with dark thread. This was the katabasis: the decline of the family expressed in the topography of her face.

So instead of returning straight to my Zurich hotel, I did in fact go to the bar of the Kronenhalle, where the door always did exactly the opposite of what one expected. If you wanted to pull it, it could only be opened with a push, and vice versa. I took my seat there in the back, down at the farthest end of the bar on the right, over by the toilets; the tables at front were always reserved for Zurich bullies and their mostly Korean female retinue. It had been a very long time since I'd gotten a table up front; they were always reserved, but not for me. I'd since given up hoping for one.

People visiting Zurich tended to think that the spirit of Joyce or of the Cabaret Voltaire would waft about them, but in reality, it was merely a city of moneygrubbing middle management and depressing hustlers and reserve lieutenants. At the bar in the back, right by the toilets, it was just as nice; at least you'd get the same three white saucers of salted almonds, paprika chips, and little pretzel sticks with your drink as at the tables up front, and if one day even that were no longer the case, one could still go to Kronenhalle's bar, because it didn't matter anyway.

Nothing mattered for my mother either. She may well have fallen on her face at her apartment again just now, tonight, depending on whether she had taken Ambien, phenobarbital, or Seroquel, meaning any one of the three drugs or all three at once, washed down with one or two of those very bottles of fendant for seven francs fifty. Then—after the fall and the footprints in the pool of blood and the neighbors' embarrassed faces behind their gossamer curtains and the white-orange ambulance and the emergency admission to the hospital and the subsequent readmission to Winterthur as well as the release a week later because there was no court order and the taxi ride back to Zurich, after which the driver would lift a thousand-franc bill from her wallet and give her no change but would instead offer his gallant arm to accompany her to the apartment door—then she would remember nothing anyway, except of course that she had a pressing need to drop off a prescription at the pharmacy for yet more packs of Ambien, phenobarbital, and Seroquel.

On my previous visit, I had scrupulously mopped up my mother's blood from the marble floor with a bucket, a cleaning rag, and a wet washcloth, after which she'd become convinced that I must have slept in her bed and not at the hotel, that the hotel was all a lie, and she'd asked how I dared bleed into her bed and on the floor like that, the nerve of it, what in God's name had gotten into me.

Anyway, there I was, sitting in the Kronenhalle bar, while she was sleeping in her apartment and I was resisting going back to my hotel, yet knowing I had to because, well, what was I even doing here at this bar that so attracted and repulsed me?

So I walked back across the bridge under which the clear river Limmat was flowing out of the lake and the swans had tucked their crowns beneath their wings to sleep. I considered standing at the wall up in the Lindenhof for a few more minutes and perhaps smoking a cigarette among the falling foliage and gazing down on the darkening city of Zurich and its gloom, which I did not do, and instead I was standing outside the hotel entrance searching my pockets for the key, for reception was no longer staffed so late at night, when, suddenly and unexpectedly, my thoughts turned to my mother's father.

And I saw the collection of sadomasochistic paraphernalia

discovered after his death, in the bolted wardrobe of the guest room in his home on the island of Sylt, that tawdry arsenal of degradation which this old man, my grandfather—party member since 1928, *Untersturmführer* in the SS and employed by the *Reichspropagandaleitung* of the Nazis in Berlin—had gathered in his home on Sylt after the war and after the, alas, complete failure of his denazification process in the British internment camp Delmenhorst-Adelheide, and which he had made use of, if not in reality, then most certainly in sweaty reverie, during clandestine cellar trysts with the young au pairs he hired from Iceland. For only they, this old man, my grandfather, had thought, could adequately represent the Nordic ideal. The Norwegians, the Germans, the Danes were too weak—no, it had to be Icelanders, girls whom he would invite to his home as au pairs, to Sylt, girls in whose blood the sacred Edda sang eternally.

Had he ever managed, back then, to have himself debased by those Icelanders living with him for years on end? One of them I could recall in great detail, a girl named Sigríður. She had been about nineteen, tall, flaxen-haired, with Kyrgyz epicanthal folds, delicate freckles on her excessively pale skin. It was with Sigríður, hunched over the desk, the tips of their tongues in the corners of their mouths, that he pored over runes, that Nordic alphabet in which the German stewards of the Nordic race were able to read the past and the future of humanity: the entirety of that esoteric drivel was explored amid the piles of books crowding my grandfather's study.

Everything: Nazi flying saucers, Antarctic New Swabia, the World Ice Theory, and of course the SS expedition to Tibet, which my grandfather had helped organize as the liaison, so to speak, between the *Reichspropagandaleitung* and *SS Ahnenerbe*—all of this silliness was discussed with patient Sigríður while eating shrimp toast and drinking lemonade and waiting for the family to go upstairs to bed already because then perhaps, at last, would come that longed-for opportunity to be tied to the table leg with barbed wire by young, pale, freckled Sigríður. *Já, elskan mín*, she might have said. *Come over here, little man.*

Sometimes, often, I'd told myself, really, it wasn't an indication of mental health to be able to adapt to such a deeply disturbed family. And how I had ever succeeded, how it had even been possible to succeed in extricating myself from my family's misery and mental illness, from these abysses that couldn't have been more profound or unfathomable or miserable, and in becoming a halfway normal human being—this I was incapable of puzzling out as I lay on the hotel bed in Zurich staring at the ceiling, while outside, beneath my window, intoxicated Zurich youths caterwauled and celebrated their depressing intoxication.

My mother may have been thoroughly objectionable, and her case, as I said, completely hopeless, but maybe, just maybe, she had been able to maintain decency in her delirium. Maybe she was firmly pursuing some new objective known only to her. Maybe she saw the future with different eyes. Or maybe she was simply afraid, as she was when she'd last called me, five years earlier, prior to the operation on her spine, and cried—though she never ever cried otherwise—and said she was so terribly afraid.

That was a moment I have never forgotten. I was standing in front of Balthazar in New York, it was spring, and people were streaming up Broadway, and I'd tried to soothe her over the telephone. You know, I told her, it's just going to be a little procedure, and so forth, but she had of course known, as she always knew everything in advance, that it would be the end of her normal life, that there would be complications after the operation, that the constant abdominal pains she'd already suffered when I was a small child would now manifest as a catastrophic infection dragging on for decades.

An infection which only surfaced after her spinal surgery, and which so strained her diminished resistance that she fell into a coma, had to be put on a ventilator through a tracheotomy, and thus lay vegetating for months in the ICU of the private clinic near Zurich, connected to various tubes, surrounded by pumping machines and grotesquely wheezing devices, by more or less well-meaning nurses and attending physicians who did their best not to let her die. This was in fact unusual in Switzerland, which has always had a special relationship with death.

In Switzerland one has the right to die, she had always

said, and that's what the doctors kept telling me as well. Even the clinic's ethics committee told me that, advising that I give consent for them to cease further treatment, to just turn the little plastic valve on the morphine tube up a bit, because how was she to recover from this, what kind of life would that be in the end? And really, life—what was that?

I, however, I found myself unable to let them do it, for I saw my mother in a Pucci bikini at the pool in St.-Jean-Cap-Ferrat whenever I closed my eyes, and not there on the gurney with that obscene tube jutting from the incision in her throat, beneath her wrinkled chin. And of course she woke up again, woke from her coma one morning as though nothing had happened, and a few weeks later she returned home in a taxi.

She'd always told me, my mother, that she could no longer swim in Lake Zurich, ever since Margie Jürgens, her best friend, had employed the Swiss company Exit for her assisted suicide and decreed that her ashes then be strewn over the clear, pleasant waters of the lake. My mother had said she'd swallow a bit of lake water by accident while swimming, and then she'd be drinking Margie, and that was a ghastly notion to her. That's not even possible, I would always reply, because how many original molecules of Margie were in a tiny sip of Lake Zurich? This wasn't at all about the actual amount, she'd always say, it was about the spirit one would ingest, not about the physical ashes, but about the immaterial. About the shadow of her best friend who would live on inside her, and that was something she couldn't bear.

And I remembered, while continuing to stare up at the ceiling of the hotel room in Zurich, my telephone call decades earlier with Margie, who'd wanted to sell me her house after the death of her husband, their beach shack, as she called it, on Great Harbour Cay in the Bahamas, where Curd had always felt so at home. A simple wooden house, hammered together out of planks, it had been their—Margie and Curd's—salvation, as she'd put it on the phone. The price they wanted for it I can't recall, but it wasn't much, even back then. I'd hesitated, however, or maybe didn't return the call because I was living in Asia at the time and the wooden house on Great Harbour Cay seemed too far away, as if located in a different, inaccessible world.

I remembered staying in Curd and Margie's villa in St.-Paul-de-Vence: the fragrant lemon groves, the cloying sweet of jasmine, a song by Harry Belafonte or Nat King Cole called "Perfidia." My father had always loved Harry Belafonte so very much, but no, I thought, no, it'd probably been Nat King Cole on the old Dual tape recorder on the marble side table, in the shade of the stone pines, who had sung *Perfidia, la perfidia de tu amor.*

And then I remembered the dark blue, almost purple cypress-lined hills in the distance, and my godfather, Eduard Rhein, whose given name I bore, half in pride, half in shame, between my own given and surnames. Eduard Rhein, who would drive up to Curd and Margie's villa in his silver Corvette, waving, with one hand on the wheel, and who had told me I must always greet him with a kiss on each cheek, he was so fond of being kissed on both cheeks, wasn't he, he was also enslaved by that song, "La Perfidia de tu Amor."

When my godfather, Eduard Rhein, later died, they found in his flat on the Croisette in Cannes an electrically adjustable, priceless tapestry, and when they flipped the switch, the wall hanging slowly rose, and behind it they discovered a secret room filled with sadomasochistic equipment, just as there had been at the home of my mother's father, only in more sumptuous finishes: twenty-four-karat golden dildos, for instance, cascades of chains, pretty gas masks, and eyeless hoods in black velvet and steel. Did my father know of that room behind the tapestry on the Croisette? Had he perhaps been inside it once himself? Had he touched those chains?

The American Field Service sent my father, Christian, to America after the war to learn about democracy and bring it back to ravaged Germany, and he sent home quite obviously faked photos: of his graduation from the University of Montana at Missoula, for instance. In those black-and-white pictures, he can be seen standing in front of a dignified bookcase in his black academic robes, a mortarboard, also in black, crowning his slender, handsome head. He sent those photographs, inscribed in pencil on the reverse, to his mother in Hamburg—my paternal grandmother, whom I never got to know.

I had once inquired: the University of Montana held no records of his ever having studied there, let alone graduated. Neither the alumni association nor the university archives found a Christian Kracht. There were also photos that showed him at his fake job at the *San Francisco Chronicle*. Then he'd returned to Germany, into the benevolent clutches of Eduard Rhein and British Major George Clare, whose parents had been murdered in Auschwitz and who worked in the denazification bureau in Hamburg as liaison officer to the newly emergent, democratic German press and who committed Axel Springer to eternal friendship with Israel, an effort that so repulsed many SS alumni that they went off to Rudolf Augstein's *Der Spiegel* magazine instead.

My father and Augstein often sat together in their favorite restaurant, Mühlenkamper Fährhaus. Each only ever ordered the *Schlemmerschnitte*—caviar and steak tartare on thickly buttered black bread—which, Augstein claimed, Hans Albers had always eaten there before the war. To accompany it Augstein drank ice-cold glasses of Linie aquavit, my father mineral water.

My father always told me that if I wanted to know the truth, I ought to speak with his friend Ralph Giordano; he was in the know about everything. After all, Giordano was the only one to have preserved civility for himself and for the Germans. And so I sought out Giordano in his high-rise apartment in Cologne to have him explain to me the state of affairs in postwar Germany, especially the integration of SS alumni into every sector of West German society, be it politics, business, journalism, intelligence services, or advertising. And Giordano, with his silk scarf and muttonchops like Lampedusa's Leopard, talked for five hours and then sent me in turn to Major Clare, in England.

Major George Clare, whom I visited at his modest home in Suffolk a few months later, was wearing an English pilot's watch from Longines, a watch with a black face secured to a green, slowly disintegrating fabric band that he carefully unfastened from his wrist with slender fingers and held out to me, saying I should take it, please, it was for me. He also gave me his two books, *Last Waltz in Vienna* and *Berlin Days*, inscribing them with a fountain pen, its sharp feather nib scratching his and my names onto the first page of each, while outside the window in the garden the English rain softly misted the roses.

Thus were we bound to each other, Major George Clare and I, whereas Eduard Rhein had given me, his newborn godson, golden cups and golden sets of cutlery and a tea service, also of twenty-four-karat gold, fashioned by the jeweler Wilm in Hamburg, engraved with my name, and it seemed to me that behind this disproportionate largesse must have lain some vile, unspeakable secret whose meaning was forever to remain hidden from me.

Whenever I later turned over the wristwatch and read the inscription *Für Georg Klaar von seinem Vater Ernst*— that had been George Clare's name in Austria—then I felt and glimpsed something that my golden cup from Eduard Rhein lacked: a context. This mug lacked the story of a Jew whose parents had been murdered, who had fled to England, had fought against the Germans, and had then returned to rebuild that country. My christening cup was, by contrast, merely a boastful golden thing the size of a beer stein, trivial. I did not understand it, nor would I ever. George Clare's wristwatch seemed a sacred relic, but Eduard Rhein's golden cup was merely an expression of avarice, a tool of deception, dead matter, dead gold—like everything in our family, dead and soulless.

That was also true of our summer home in St.-Jean-Cap-Ferrat, which my father had bought off Eduard Rhein, but also of the chalet in Gstaad, which had previously belonged to Karim Aga Khan. Everything was closely and inseparably interconnected. The golden cutlery and the various houses; the collection of German expressionists and the unsavory instruments of torture; the SS expedition to Tibet and my mother's protracted decline; the private Zurich banks, the conservative German press, and the shell corporations in Panama and Jersey.

It was as if for decades I'd been trailing along the verge of enormous malice and was simply unable to make it out, as if within my assumptions lay only further assumptions, as if I'd been stricken by a disease of the morphic field, a cruel perfidy radiating from the past. As if it had been put into my mind that the circumstances of my childhood and youth were in some way special or extraordinary, when in reality they were steeped not only in bourgeois mediocrity—for that I'd have been able to accept—but also in profound menace.

If only I could read some ancient chronicle—the book of world memory perhaps, or the South Indian palm-leaf manuscripts—I'd know everything, I'd be able to understand, in an instant, all the connections that had remained hidden. For example, the repeated rapes, stretching over weeks, of my then eleven-year-old mother by a bicycle shop owner in Itzehoe, a town in Holstein, who made her swear an oath never to testify against him, after my grandfather had suspected the assaults and pressed charges, or else she would never get the pretty children's bike he had promised her. The charges were dismissed because the bicycle shop owner was a cousin of Itzehoe's Nazi mayor, Kurt Petersen, who had remained in office until the end of the war and, in the small hours of Sunday, April 3, 1949, attempted suicide along with his wife by ingesting—what else?—phenobarbital.

So that had taken place in 1949, when my grandfather had already returned from denazification and immediately set about reactivating his network of old SS *Kameraden*. His daughter had been raped, and the *Kameraden* would come to visit. And that name Petersen shot through everything like a treacherous key to understanding, while in reality it only clouded thought, the name Petersen. There was, I recalled, the painter Wilhelm Petersen, also *Untersturmführer* in the

SS, whose self-illustrated book *Danse Macabre in Poland* lay henceforth on my grandfather's end table, beside the bottle of egg liqueur and the two tiny crystal glasses, next to the worn leather wingback chair in which my grandfather himself sat, his snow white hair combed back severely, his hands folded calmly before him, humming an old melody which only he remembered—the one about wild geese that sweep through the night sky, in which the world is full of murder—while he, my grandfather, patiently awaited the sonorous gong on television that signaled the start of the evening news.

My grandfather, my mother's father, had been personal assistant to Horst Dressler-Andress, director of the Central Office for Radio and cofounder of Kraft durch Freude, who, after his arrest by the Soviets, had been able to get across to them through dialectical argument that he had essentially been a socialist within National Socialism and never in a million years a fascist. Thus he was not immediately put up against the wall or deported to Siberia but released, promoted, and courted. Dressler-Andress launched an unprecedented career in East Germany, especially as a politician for the National-Democratic Party, a cesspit of former Nazi Party members, and he was ultimately awarded the Order of Merit of East Germany. Upon reunification in 1990, however, the National-Democratic Party and its members were absorbed, one and all, into the Free Democrats—also the favored party of my grandfather in Kampen on Sylt, and the party of painter Wilhelm Petersen as well.

It was this very same Wilhelm Petersen who had made the paintings and drawings that hung on the walls of my grandfather's thatched-roof home in Kampen. One of his most famous works was actually called *Es reitet der Tod*, or *Death Comes a-Riding*. This then was what I'd been surrounded by as a child: on one side, my father's German expressionists, which is to say the degenerate artists, and on my mother's side, SS artists who painted pictures they titled *Es reitet der Tod*.

Wilhelm Petersen had been a war artist for the SS, expressly appointed by Heinrich Himmler, whose personal staff he joined. Later, following the war, when understandably enough no one wanted to commission paintings from Petersen anymore, my godfather, Eduard Rhein, tasked him with drawing an invention of his, the children's book character Mecki, a whimsical, slightly annoying hedgehog. In those books, which paired SS racial doctrine with an insufferable petit bourgeois mentality, in works like *Mecki bei den Negerlein*, the faces of the Africans Mecki visited were the most dim-witted, racist caricatures. Africans, wearing only grass skirts, stuck wooden spoons and whisks through their earlobes and spouted pathetic, savage inanities.

An African school appeared in that Mecki book, which in turn called to mind the time my grandfather, one evening in Kampen when things weren't proceeding in their usual orderly manner—something or other was cluttering the carpet, or everyone had dared to speak at once—suddenly shouted, *It's like being at the Jew school here!* That was the only violent outburst I'd ever experienced from my grandfather. To me it had seemed as if the fabric of reality were breached, and I hid myself away, trembling with fear, in the guest room underneath the thatched roof. The same guest room in which my grandfather's collection of children's books, consisting largely of works by Fritz Baumgarten, provided comfort and refuge. In the thirties, Baumgarten had dreamed up and drawn an anthropomorphic world—as in the Mecki universe, except *before* the Second World War—in which various songbirds, imps, and teddy bears frolicked about and sang German folk songs together, and beneath the surface, it seemed to me even then as a child, something creepy and dark was going on. As if concealing itself within those drawings by Fritz Baumgarten—genial, portending safety and comfort—was the baleful German soul, entwined in shadows.

It was the guest room in whose always locked wardrobe the implements of abuse would be found thirty years later, after the death of my grandfather, at whose funeral his wife, my grandmother, bearer of the bronze Cross of Honor of the German Mother for the five children she'd given to the Führer—among them my mother—had fallen to her knees at the open grave in Kampen and, weeping, let forth a heart-rending scream. *Just wait*, she called, altering the words of that Icelandic au pair Sigríður. *Just wait, sweet husband, soon I'll come down to you in the grave.*

Also in Kampen, on that island of Sylt, several streets away, the publisher Peter Suhrkamp had sold his house, likewise roofed in thatch, to Axel Springer, in order to afford the German translation rights for Proust's *In Search of Lost Time*, which today seems to me a very good trade. In Springer's house, too, I'd frequently slept in a room right under the roof, where at night, when I didn't want to venture out into the corridor to visit the bathroom, I peed into the washbasin affixed to the wall—so often that the sink began to emit an acrid smell, and I poured lye and detergent and men's cologne into it to mask the stench. I was afraid Axel Springer would fire my father when he found out that I had been peeing into his sink. For my father always stayed in Springer's house when he was on Sylt, because he had always hated his parents-in-law. They'd been Nazis, he said, and were still Nazis, and he refused even to speak to them, and so he would always stay with us at Axel Springer's when he was on Sylt, never in my grandfather's house a little farther down the road toward the dunes, right around where Göring had once lost his dagger in the beach grass. For everything that does not rise into consciousness will return as fate.

And so, back in the closed psychiatric ward in Winterthur, while my mother's eightieth birthday guests were looking for the exit, she was taken back to her tiny room, her cell, her bed, her chair, her barred window. And there, she experienced a sudden alertness, she hadn't seen or spoken to her siblings in twenty years, she became lucid, and as I sat by her bedside and gently held her hands, she told me about the bicycle shop owner in Itzehoe who had raped her.

With total calm, in the reluctant, quiet words of a child, she told me what had happened to her in 1949 at age eleven in northern Germany, in Itzehoe. She had been raped, again and again, and at this I cried, cried and took her in my arms, and told her that she was safe now, here in Winterthur on the closed psychiatric ward, and that she didn't need to be afraid anymore, and that something similar had happened to me, also when I was eleven, only in 1979, at my Canadian boarding school. Yes, she had always known about that, and had believed me, she said, even back then—she was just incapable of talking about it, ever, the pain prevented her, the pain of her own abuse and the shame of having been unable to prevent it for her own child, precisely three decades later.

My goodness, this life, what a perfidious, sordid, miserable melodrama it was, I thought, while continuing to stare at the ceiling of the hotel room, realizing that this was in fact the eternal return, our inability to pinpoint any beginning of time—*aeternitas a parte ante*, as a priest in Florence had once tried to explain it to me. Should one ever succeed in interrupting the cycle of history, one could influence not only the future but the past as well.

. . . .

And then I no longer saw my mother, but Elsie von Oehrli. She'd been my nanny, part of an age-old lineage of noble-women from the Bernese Oberland. She had grayish white hair tied at the back in a bun, and little diamond studs in her earlobes, and crow's-feet around her eyes, and pretty freckles on her face, and she was to me the first beautiful woman who wasn't my mother: German, clear, and cold.

Elsie von Oehrli had lived down the road, at the bend leading down to the Palace Hotel in Gstaad. She had sung to me when my parents were out of town, when I stayed at her chalet and was allowed to sleep in her bed with her and turn the dial on her brown radio to Minsk and Beromünster and RIAS Berlin. And when there were no more nighttime programs, after two o'clock in the morning, in Elsie's arms I listened to the infinite series of numbers declaimed monotonously on the long-wave station. *Fünnef, sieben, acht, eins, fünnef, zwo, zwo, fünnef, neun, fünnef*: mystical, eerie series of numbers. They were coded messages sent to us at night to Switzerland from the Soviet Zone, and I felt an indeterminate fear of these voices on the radio.

Elsie had said I needn't be afraid, ever, and she sang to me *Roti Rösli im Garte / Meierisli im Wald / Wenn dä Wind chunt cho blase / So verwelked sie bald*, and she clutched my hand in the night and held me as I slept. Her curtains were of embroidered linen. The floor in her bedroom was splintery wood, and in her little garden white roses blossomed along the wooden fence. And she herself smelled as clean and pure as the freshly washed white sheets on the line, dried by the warm *foehn* wind blowing down the Glacier des Diablerets and through the valley to us.

At this I fell asleep and did not dream for a long time, and as soon as I awoke the next morning I remembered the paper bag and the sweater inside it I had purchased the previous evening on Bahnhofstrasse. I got up, went to the bathroom, and cleaned my teeth. Then I sat on the edge of the bed, removed the sweater from the bag, and buried my face in it. It smelled earthy, like hay and damp wool, like dog and sawdust and dry leaves. And the way it smelled and felt was such that I slipped on the sweater over bare skin and hugged myself before the hotel-room mirror, as I had always done long ago, in front of the mirrors of my childhood.

II.

I had always lived in dreams, among the ghosts of language. Never have I understood why, after leaving Switzerland at eleven to attend Canadian boarding school, I always needed to shift around the globe afterward, my belongings carried with me in plastic bags and hard-shell suitcases or else stashed away somewhere in various storage units. CDs that could no longer be listened to because there were no more CD players. Records that could no longer be played because there were no more turntables. Books consumed by termites and dampness, and clothing that had become unfashionable and moldy.

Why out of some disturbed need peculiar to me I had to live in Bangkok and Florence and Buenos Aires, in California and Sri Lanka and Kenya and India and Kyoto for years at a time, why I had to rent and buy homes and apartments abroad, why I was raising a child who remembered being able to understand Swahili, being able to understand Italian, being able to understand Hindi, being able to understand French, being able to understand Swiss German, being able to understand Spanish, and being able to understand Argentine Castilian, that soft, limp Spanish with the *shsh* sounds. Why, I did not know.

A child who took enjoyment not only in speaking Italian with a Russian accent, speaking Saxon with an Indian accent, speaking French with a Scottish accent, but also in the scarcely perceptible tonal nuances of language, of High German with a Basel accent, of Glaswegian with a Punjabi accent, of Texan with a Tuscan accent, as though in such acoustic outgrowths, in such minimal shifts among linguistic molecules, something might be detected, gleaned by listening, which would then divide sounds according to truth and fabrication, which would classify them as original and copy.

It was always language itself, the liberation and simultaneous domination of the spastic glottis, that singular enigma which lay in the proper sequence of syllables. And it was always, then, the German. It had always been the German language. It had always been the scorched earth, the sufferings of ill-treated earth itself, war and the burning old city and the vegetable fields made infertile outside it. It had always been the ghetto purged with the flamethrower. It had always been the tailored, pale gray uniforms, the attractive blond officers with their ice-cube-filled gullets, whispering, smiling. It had always been the girl's dark brown hair pinned on the left by that barrette, a curtain before her face brushed aside gently by her hand; it had always been the candle extinguished in Amsterdam.

. . . .

I lived in the past, the last twenty-five, thirty-five years, which likewise felt as though they hadn't just transpired but were eternally present. The past was always much more real and elastic and present than the now. I lived in films. And I lived in cinemas, I slept in cinemas. And the cinemas were shut down or relocated to shopping malls in municipal hinterlands, which people had begun to call *Agglos*. Where cinemas had once been, boutiques now moved in, selling coats and purses and shoes no one needed or deemed beautiful except for my mother, pieces from Loro Piana, for instance, or checkered, quilted blazers from Ferragamo or low-heeled shoes from Tod's.

This unopened stuff, the sweaters and cardigans and blankets and pleated slacks my mother bought in these boutiques, had wandered into the armoires of her apartment, stacked and stowed away and archived, where they sat, never looked at again, next to dozens of Hermès handbags and the hundreds of Ferragamo shoes that were never worn. The furs, sable and silver fox and the like, that had not been stolen by the housekeeper were divided among five storage units my mother maintained in Zurich because it was no longer appropriate to wear furs, but neither could they be thrown out, just as nothing at all could ever really be thrown out, because everything does have a history, you know.

So even those never unwrapped, compulsively bought articles of clothing were a part of history, a part of her obsession following her experiences of the war and the postwar years. It was as if history had manifested its own fetishes, which then vanished within the dimness of my mother's armoire. They had become enchanted objects whose meaning had been lost forever.

What might my mother have seen, as a small child, in those final war years? Had she seen deserters being strung up from lampposts with cardboard signs around their necks? Had she seen body parts hanging from the bombed-out buildings, their façades open like dollhouses? Had she seen missing walls, had she peeked into these oversized dollhouse parlors, had she seen those crushed limbs, beset by flies and maggots, severed by the force of the exploding bombs, had she seen liquefied bodies and human organs spattered about, torrents of refugees moving westward, mown down by machine gun fire from low-flying fighter planes, barns burning, wheat fields burning, churches burning—what had she been forced to see with her own eyes in the mangled wasteland of her childhood?

And why did my father always have to buy houses in places where he hoped for a connection to a society that would never otherwise have welcomed him? He had now been dead a decade, my father. The flat on Upper Brook Street in London's Mayfair district. The chalet of Aga Khan in Gstaad. The villa in Cap Ferrat, situated on the bluff between Somerset Maugham's home and the king of Belgium's estate. The house in Kampen on Sylt. The house in Sea Island, Georgia. And finally the château in Morges on Lake Geneva, where he had died.

I was fond of recalling this house, this somewhat meek version of the Rothschilds' Château de Pregny. I still see the faded baroque of the van Dyck in the entrance hall, which in the time between two of my visits had been removed from the paneling, likely cut out, rolled up, and sent off to Sotheby's. There was always a very direct link between art and money—never the slightest doubt that they belonged together and were as one.

In my mind's eye I saw the sofas upholstered with golden silk in the grand salon and, perched on the edge of one of them, my father in his pale gray English flannel suit, narrow shoes on his slender feet. I saw his cunning, icy bright eyes. His gaze traveled out far over the park, past Lake Geneva to Evian and on to the French Alps, orange-red and yielding in the dusk. I saw the furnishings of his dressing room, lined up to the ceiling in fawn and orange leathers by Hermès, with hundreds of shallow teak drawers, one for each bespoke dress shirt from Harvie and Hudson. Then the pair of early expressionist paintings by Lyonel Feininger, the one titled *Jesuits*, the other *The Newspaper Readers*, hanging above the desk in the study paneled in mahogany and teak. The collection of hundreds of diaphanous Chinese teacups he'd amassed over decades, like Chatwin's Kaspar Utz, who suffered from that incurable porcelain sickness. But why all this?

I knew from the moment I guessed what it was all worth that not only would I never be able to live like that, but that my childhood and youth were permeated by arrogance and hyperbole and fraud and degradation, by dead money. It was my father's fear of provinciality, of his own humble origins, that emanated from him even after his death. His father had been a taxi driver, in Hamburg, with everything that entails. The nightly bar crawl the little boy had to go along for, his father's dull, inebriated, violent blows, the post-Wilhelmine mercilessness of the lower classes. That was a place he never wanted to go back to, whatever the cost.

And so after the war he minced into the milieu of Axel Springer. He met the right people while wearing the right suits, though at first they were still sewn from the rough, scratchy fabric of the blackout blankets. He made quite an impression with his elegant demeanor and his nefariousness. For Springer, who'd received a license to print newspapers from the British, he procured whole truck convoys full of paper rolls on the black market. He was on the rise, ever upward, until he became the powerful publisher's right hand.

He had tried living in England, tried working himself in at the very top in bespoke suits from Davies and Son, the same company on Savile Row that tailored Axel Springer's clothing. He wore custom-made shoes from John Lobb with gently elevated heels because his slightness embarrassed him; he was a short, slender man. He socialized in the right London clubs, he lived exclusively in the districts of Mayfair and Belgravia, he loved England, but they had not let him in. Although he learned that during luncheon at Simpson's in the Strand one must slip a few coins into the white-aproned breast pocket of the carver who rolled the silver roast beef cart over to the table, the stink of the German working class still clung to my father's bespoke English suits, as did the affectations of a parvenu.

There was so much he didn't understand, my father. The issue of reverse snobbery, for example, and of Belgravia Cockney, *the final vulgarity of the English upper class*. And then the tailored shirts whose collars had to be tattered and full of holes. They had to be foxed, just about to fall apart in fact. Nor did he understand how to wear suede ankle boots, known as chukkas, which had to be perfectly unsightly: scuffed and stained as though the wearer had tramped through multiple puddles the day before and then forgotten to clean them. My father lacked self-irony, he wasn't pukka, he had simply not been the right man, like Barry Lyndon. It wasn't about money or influence or anything; no, it just wasn't enough to come from Hamburg and to want to be an Englishman.

He had secretly fathered a son with an Englishwoman in the English countryside, in Suffolk or Somerset or somewhere else. Sometimes he would return home to Gstaad after one or two months away and tell stories about the modest English farm where he'd been: the sheep in the enclosure, the apple trees and the dovecote, the plain food and plain goodness of the country people. I recall thinking as a child that we lived in the countryside here in Gstaad though, too. Our neighbors were all farmers as well. Their cows laid their heads on the fence outside my bedroom window and woke me every morning with their bells. I even had to drink their gross fresh milk for breakfast, still warm. It was every bit as much a country life as in England, I thought at the time, but of course I never said a word—I never said anything against my father. Our relationship consisted of a total affirmation of his feudalistic being. It was never possible to be of a different mind. At no time had this been possible. You fell in line, agreed with him, and received money for it.

And when he died, my stepmother, his last wife, took the Learjet from Geneva to the memorial service in Hamburg, on her lap the long coveted thirty-five-thousand-euro Birkin handbag that my father had always forbidden her to own. Inside, inside this Hermès purse, lay his ashes, in a plastic bag, ashes she later hurled from a tugboat off Hamburg-Finkenwerder into the river Elbe: both the plastic bag and the ashes into the filthy Elbe.

I can see it now, the swaying barge, the jaundiced two-hundred-euro bill hastily and bashfully presented so that the drunk captain would turn a blind eye, the mute, absolutely petrified family on the quarterdeck, the milky Hamburg sky, the plastic bag sinking slowly in the boat's wake, the squawking, diving, horrid seagulls.

My mother of course had not been invited to the memorial

service, which concluded with a family dinner at Hamburg's Hotel Vier Jahreszeiten. We had been seated in a private back room, in neckties and in silence, an awkward silence expressly desired by my stepmother, and disturbed only by the bevy of liveried waiters who announced and described the gimmicky roundelay of courses in advance. It was abysmally, depressingly bourgeois, these loudly and proudly proclaimed lobster tails on pea essence, these Chateaubriands, these basil sorbets.

After the meal I'd stepped out in front of the nocturnally illuminated hotel to smoke a cigarette. No guests had been invited; Ralph Giordano learned of my father's death from the newspapers. And when I had crumpled up the slips of paper with the Yeats poem and the eulogy I hadn't read aloud and tossed them into a trash can, my father's Hamburg attorney had suddenly appeared behind me and put an amicable arm around my shoulder, assuring me that he was always there for me if I needed him. Really, always. And then he had pinched me on the upper flesh of my shoulder, in the Hanseatic manner. I should have yelled at him had I not been so cowardly.

What had my father even done during the war? He'd been born back in 1921, making him prime soldier stock. On the internet it says he was with an infantry regiment and was wounded. That information about him can't have been right, though. He'd never mentioned anything of the sort.

Wounded by whom? And more to the point, where? He'd always said he was supposed to be sent to the Eastern Front, which prompted his best friend, staff surgeon Günter Kelch, to plunge him into the ice-cold Elbe to help him contract pneumonia, and then inject his arm with typhoid pathogens, so that, deathly ill and highly infectious, he would not be shipped east. He was a Social Democrat his whole life long, he'd always claimed, he hated the Nazis, and after the war he had in fact been in the United States, with the American Field Service. Well, whatever the case, my father's smallish lies were nothing next to the established truths of my mother's family.

Anyway, his friend, staff surgeon Günter Kelch, had been homosexual, had loved Zarah Leander more than anything, and was present throughout my entire childhood. My father had always said Günter—whom we were supposed to call Güntimäusi, Günter Mouse—had saved his life in the war by injecting him with typhoid, and that he must now take care of him; that was his sacred duty. My father paid Günter Kelch an allowance, as he was unable to hold a job of any kind due to his advanced alcoholism. He was always being kicked out of everywhere, and my father clothed him, mostly in Axel Springer's bespoke suits, purloined for him in Kampen on Sylt, since both men, Axel and Güntimäusi, had the same elegant build: tall and slender and chiseled.

So Güntimäusi, for whom my father bankrolled a little flat not far from Rothenbaumchaussee in Hamburg, loved dancing for me and my mother in women's clothing. We knew all the songs of Marlene Dietrich, of Zarah Leander, by heart, but the song about the Fiji Islands *Ich lass' mir meinen Körper schwarz bepinseln* was Güntimäusi's favorite, as were *Yes, Sir* and *Lili Marleen* and *Ich weiß, es wird einmal ein Wunder geschehen* and of course *Waldemar*.

My father had had an affair with Inge Feltrinelli, whose husband Giangiacomo, an Italian publisher with ever-deepening connections to militant leftist extremism, was killed at the beginning of the seventies in a dynamite attack.

Axel Springer's chalet near Gstaad was set on fire, as was his second estate, on the island of Sylt, the Klenderhof. Incidentally, our chalet in Gstaad also burned down, after my father had sold it to Mick and Muck Flick. Our houses had always burned down, and I always wondered what that was supposed to mean. Perhaps my mother knew.

As a small child I would often stand in fear before a painting that hung in our chalet above the wooden staircase to the second floor. It was by some Dutchman, with a very small burning farm in Flanders visible in the background. I was unable to remember anything more, maybe snow, probably crows circling in a pallid overcast winter sky as well, people dressed in black coming from the left and walking into the image. Today I have the sense that it must have been Pieter Bruegel's *Hunters in the Snow* hanging on our wall, which I saw once more decades later in the Kunsthistorisches Museum in Vienna.

In any event, fire had always been inside me: the house fire, the glowing remains of the chalets, and the Marie-José primary school in Gstaad I had set ablaze, the Polaroids presented to me as a seven-year-old in juvenile court in Thun to prove what I had done. The photos had shown a scorched chalkboard eraser, roof timbering gutted by fire, scattered matches charred black along half their length, their tips curled onto themselves like tiny, shrunken heads. There had been a half-empty green bottle of lighter fluid, the beige paper of its label frayed, then insulating material torn from the rafters, shredded in a corner of the attic, stacked, and ignited. Photos I still see in my dreams to this day, like discarded, inadequate rejects from Andrei Tarkovsky's Polaroid collection. Almost half a century ago, radiating European world.

III.

As I unpacked the sweater, the pamphlet had slid from the bag onto the carpet. I picked it up and leafed through it while getting dressed. I was still at the hotel in Zurich. *Join us at the vegetarian Dirk Hamer Commune*, the awkwardly titled brochure read, showing photos of blond Swiss families cultivating their fields, making pottery together, and picking apples, all in desaturated colors.

A phone number was listed; you were to call if you wished to come by, you needn't bring anything except the desire to work together fairly according to your ability. First and foremost, they operated equitably. You might also do nothing at all for a start and then maybe, once you felt like it, you might help shear sheep whose wool would then be gently processed into sweaters at the commune. Instead of throwing the brochure into the waste basket, I folded it and slipped it into my jacket pocket.

Then I went downstairs to the breakfast area, ate a croissant and drank three cups of black coffee, read the local section of the *Neue Zürcher Zeitung*, and walked over the cobblestones in the morning sun to the nearby florist to buy a few champagne-colored roses. Today I only asked for nineteen, not thirty-five like two months ago, or the two dozen of months prior.

Zurich was claustrophobic; the little flower shop made me claustrophobic, the old city made me claustrophobic, the fifteenth-century buildings, never destroyed in World War II, made me claustrophobic, the ladies with their shopping bags from Kaufhaus Grieder made me claustrophobic and cut me off, the streetcars made me claustrophobic and cut me off, the bankers walking to their banks to accumulate more gold beneath Paradeplatz made me claustrophobic and cut me off. Recently, a few months earlier, I had seen a banana peel lying on the cobblestones, and I'd stood awhile to wait and see what would happen, but no one slipped on it. The residents of Zurich were of course too shrewd to slip on a banana peel. They were too superior, too confident, too steeped in that grand Zurich world of theirs, in which they shopped in boutiques whose vertiginous monthly rents continued to sustain this, their Zurich.

But then I thought that I was actually fortunate to be in Switzerland and not to have to be in Germany, where the blood of murdered Jews still stained the streets and the people were not the least bit shy about anything, although of course it would well suit them to be a little bit more introverted and humble, the Germans. A Germany whose manly Germans would shout into their manly mobile phones in public, especially when they were in Switzerland, and where it looked and sounded like they were on the phone with the

Reichspropagandaleitung, slouched and spread-eagled on the sofas of the first-class lounge at Zurich Airport, whereas in reality they were merely speaking with an ad agency or with their department manager. What luck, I thought, what luck, how lucky that I was in Switzerland.

So I walked back up the road, cellophane-enveloped flowers in hand, and hailed a taxi outside the hotel. Out toward the sun-dazzled waters, to my mother, to that hideous suburb of hers on Lake Zurich, and after giving the driver the address, I contemplated that I would by no means confront her once more with her misery today, but would instead ask her why at the time Monsieur Pierre Gruneberg absolutely had to be the one to teach me to swim.

For my mother, it had been essential that it only be him, as if by Pierre Gruneberg's touch, by this man's very presence, my life would turn toward greater things all on its own because the *maître-nageur* Gruneberg had taught the children of Frank Sinatra and David Niven in the pool at the Hotel du Cap, and that of Brigitte Bardot, who the tabloids had once claimed was married to my father, a man who, according to the same article, always left his bedroom light on at the chalet in Gstaad, because he spent his nights on the phone to the Tokyo stock exchange, increasing his vast fortune.

I recalled Pierre Gruneberg's secret command, in my memory always issued in a barely audible whisper—I must have been four or five. It was *grenouille, ciseaux, crayon*. And as I looked back on it now after all these years, this had been of course my *asa, nisi, masa*. The magical directive to draw out my child body in the salt water of that impossibly blue hotel pool first into a frog, then a pair of scissors, and then a pencil. Arms and legs had to be moved away from the body, flexed, and extended laterally. This had to be repeated a hundred times; then Pierre Gruneberg was finally satisfied, and so was my mother.

Our house in Cap Ferrat stood atop a bluff overlooking the bay of Villefranche. I remember the dark blue and yellow deck chair cushions with white piping down by the pool. I recall Hermès towels wrapped around my mother's head, lemon trees on the hillside, pine nuts you had only to pick up off the ground to eat. The mistral winds blowing all the way from the North Pole to the Côte d'Azur in winter and, once, the spectacle of the French aircraft carrier *Clemenceau*, bedecked with flags, down in the bay below our house.

Perhaps today I would really be able to speak with her. Perhaps today I would not have to take my cue from the past. Perhaps today, rather than just pretending, I would succeed in accepting her as she was, and then, for once, not vanish down the bottomless rabbit hole of memory, but be amenable to the moment, to her delusions, to which I could simply open myself. What on earth did she want?

And then the taxi was pulling up in front of the apartment complex. I dreaded this moment every time: the slow approach, coming to a halt, the vague, absurd fear of stopping in a no-stopping zone amid the reduced-traffic area of my mother's Zurich suburb, and the certainty that behind their double-glazed windows, my mother's neighbors were noting down the taxi's license plate number.

Detestably enough, people in Zurich called this area the Gold Coast, or perhaps that was what they called the opposite shore, I'd forgotten which, not that it mattered. In any case, she had been living for over twenty-five years in this depressing white faux-Bauhaus box from the early nineties, with a lake view. It was thoroughly repellent, this building on the awful Gold Coast, which might well have been the other side of Lake Zurich and not this one. I got out, paid, and buzzed once, twice. I half expected my mother not to answer, while hoping of course that she would, that she was alive and not lying in a pool of blood again.

My mother appeared, hunched crookedly, smiling, and when I gave her three kisses on alternating cheeks, she smelled just as she always did: of Ashes of Roses by Bourjois and the slightest hint of lemon. Her face was more familiar to me than any other, although in it I only ever saw the face of my young mother, meeting life with hopeful anticipation, the face of the mother I recalled from my childhood, and not her bruised, ruined face of today, puffy from vodka and phenobarbital and disappointment and pain.

. . . .

"Mama." Emphasis on the second syllable. "You're looking well."

"Only one who has lived before 1789 can possibly know how pleasant life can be," she replied. It was her favorite quote; she had read it at some point in Talleyrand, and she found it funny and applicable at all times, which I guess it was.

"Did you get some sleep at least?"

"Surely you can't be serious. I haven't slept since you were a child. I fall asleep at eleven, with pills, and wake up at half past two in the morning. You know that, my boy."

I was wondering, as I so often had before, whether she was truly well read or just acted the part, and after cutting the bottoms from the stems of the roses I had brought and dumping ice cubes into the crystal vase, I found a spot for it next to the colored-glass lamp, slid the vase a little to the left, sat on the edge of the green silk sofa, and leafed through the coffee-table books, yellowed by the now departed summer sun: books on Istanbul, on Barbara Hepworth, on Argentine estancias, on Tolstoy.

I reflected on the fact that Tiffany lamps would never again be appealing; they had been ruined for all time, these aberrant lamps, like awful Belle Époque paintings and tapered Coca-Cola bottles and ballet dancers by Degas and handblown purplish floral Murano glass figurines and those

Toulouse-Lautrec absinthe bottles. This foppery would never come back, and I was glad that my mother had nothing quite so repulsive in her apartment, except of course for the Tiffany lamps, a pair my father had given her so that he wouldn't have to hand over the Nolde *Flower Garden* painting he had promised her for her fiftieth birthday.

"I wanted to ask you something."

"You did? What? Wait, what's that awful hippie sweater you're wearing?"

A *Bunte* magazine from the April or May before last lay open on the Chinese coffee table, as though it had only just now been glanced at, not the year before, the photos of Ernst August von Hannover at Munich's Oktoberfest had almost completely faded, however, which meant no one had flipped through the *Bunte*. The magazine had been lying open for months just like that, as if time had stopped. *Bunte* was so important to my mother because it relentlessly depicted an everlasting present; a *Bunte* magazine from ten or twenty years ago evoked for her the same moment as the current issue, the moment events took place, which is to say, the time in which my mother lingered *aeternitas a parte ante*.

"Do you remember the swimming pool at the Hotel du Cap?"

"You mean in St.-Paul-de-Vence?"

"No, Mama, at the hotel, at the Hotel du Cap in Cap Ferrat."

"Well, not really."

"We had a house on the cape, next to the zoo. It was called Villa Roc Escarpé. And I was supposed to learn to swim. And one day I jumped off the side and then spun around in the air and knocked out my two front teeth on the edge of the pool when you were both away, Papa and you."

I watched the cogs slowly turning behind her pale blue eyes, saw the spark of recognition fade again. A fly wanted out, into the sunny outdoors. It quivered against the window, over and over, fatally drowsy, trapped in the apartment since the summer.

"I don't remember."

"We had a gardener named . . . uh . . . Gérard. He would come from Nice every morning on his moped. He had a black bushy mustache and smelled like machine oil. And there was a swimming teacher, over at the Hotel du Cap."

"No."

"And he would say: *grenouille, ciseaux, crayon.*"

"Yes."

"You remember that."

"Yes, child. *Grenouille, ciseaux, crayon.* Yes, that I recall. *Grenouille, ciseaux, crayon.*"

. . . .

Sometimes I had the clearly erroneous impression that in my absence she had arranged her living room just for me: the *Neue Zürcher Zeitung* here, the silver-framed photo of me as the twenty-seven-year-old author of *Faserland* in a Barbour jacket there, plus the photo of our golden retriever Daisy, dead for many years, on the faience table toward the back, with the stack of unopened bank statements over there. It was just that I was unable to grasp the meaning of the arrangement; the intent behind its order which she may have wished to convey was lost on me.

After failing as a child in my scheme to re-create the entire world out of Legos at a one-to-one ratio—not just my desk and my bed and my Lego box, but our whole chalet, the chalet of our neighbor Mohamed al-Fayed, the entire village of Gstaad and all the surrounding mountains, and finally all of Switzerland and everything else, too—I had begun wearing makeup every day as a young man (between my thirteenth and twenty-seventh birthdays to be exact, so, for fourteen years), using the products of the Coty company, Airspun Soft in particular, which gave me what I thought was a perfect, smooth complexion.

Airspun Soft was a loose setting powder, also often available in a tin as a cream. It concealed lines, wrinkles, acne, and spots, leaving behind a gorgeous, delicate, velvety flawlessness. Airspun Soft could be used for highlighting and contouring, for beautifying, or applied, as I preferred at the time, as a foundation spread thickly over my entire face. My hair was also dyed dark red with henna, and I either brushed it straight up or combed it back severely every day with shaving foam, wanting to look like John Foxx or David Sylvian in their early years. I wore beige jodhpurs and smoked colorful, very slim Russian cigarettes called Sobranies. Each morning I also drank two or three gulps of Odol mouthwash, and I shaved my armpits smooth three times a week until they bled. Then at twenty-seven, all this eccentricity ceased abruptly, because my novel *Faserland* was published.

When I was twenty-five, I recalled, I'd decided to write a novel in the first person, in which I would affect the air of an autistic snob and fool myself and the reader into thinking that I came from a good family and had suffered only from affluent neglect. Maybe it would turn into an affectionate caricature, with a dose of German romanticism in the vein of Eichendorff's *Good-for-Nothing* and a dash of French humor like in Voltaire's *Candide*. The first-person narrator, so, me, was supposed to like listening to the Eagles; I had cribbed that from Bret Easton Ellis. At the time that had made a very deep impression on me because I—the real me, I mean—actually thought the Eagles were awful, because I wore jodhpurs and hennaed hair and liquid eyeliner under my eyes and Airspun Soft by Coty on my face and smoked Sobranies, and not just the Eagles but the people who liked the Eagles, too. And so I'd written this book, in the evenings, in my one-room apartment in Hamburg, subsisting on oven-crisped pizza baguettes and toast with bland mustard and ravioli from a tin. The same apartment I vacated, by the way, when I could no longer afford it, and which my friend Olaf Dante Marx then moved into, only to die of AIDS a few weeks later. Anyway, and now I'm getting to the point, either the character or his monologues—because there was no dialogue whatsoever in the book—were so believable that the readers of *Faserland* assumed the person writing like that was the real me.

Today, though, today was apparently a good day. My mother was not yet drunk: she usually only started around midday, perhaps as early as eleven but sometimes not until two. Sometimes she wouldn't even drink until the late afternoon, when the tremblings began.

"Would you like a coffee?"

"Yes, that would be kind, please do make me a coffee."

With a soft brush, I combed her hair, which she hadn't washed in a long while. It was a gentle motion, this brushing, and she closed her eyes as though it gave her joy, and when I was done, I snapped in an amber barrette at the back.

"It's nice when you brush my hair."

"Yes."

"It feels nice," she said.

And then, after we'd sat down and I'd brewed a coffee, the perennial litany began again, that everyone was stealing from her, and why didn't I finally move in upstairs to prevent these daily robberies that made life so insufferable for a woman like her who had a reputation to lose.

"And for that matter, where's my car?" she asked. "And did you brew the coffee with Ährensonne, too, like I asked?"

"Yes, Mama."

"Which, my car or the coffee?"

"Your car is parked safely in the garage."

"Fabulous. When the canton of Zurich gives me back my license, we'll take a drive and have trout over at Sihlmatt."

"Yes. Of course. I'd like to do that with you, Mama."

"You children have always had it easy. You've always had it easy. Everyone has always had it easy."

She drank from her cup and looked at me. Her eyes were the eyes of my mother and at the same time the eyes of an insane old woman.

"Every sip is satisfaction, every sip is bliss, bar none," she said. "What Gustav Pavel crafts for us is brought to life by sheaves of sun. Ährensonne, the real ersatz coffee. You know that?"

"Yes, I know it."

It was one of her recurring memories from childhood, a marketing slogan from the time right after the war, when her

father, my grandfather, following his stint in the denazification camp, was able to employ his expertise from the
Reichspropagandaleitung at the advertising agency Lintas,
thinking up the names of bath products like Badedas and
Duschdas for them, among others. It was hard to believe,
when you really thought about it.

I see a black-and-white photograph: my mother standing
in front of a thatched-roof house in Kampen, on Sylt, probably in the early sixties, before I was born in any case, the
beach grass beside her, an Hermès scarf wrapped around
her head. She is looking straight into the camera, her hands
clenched into fists at her sides; there is a lunacy in her face,
as well as an unbridled rage at the photographer, presumably
my father.

"What do you regret most?" she asked. "Please pour me a
glass of white wine."

I went into the kitchen and opened the refrigerator. The
only things in it were individually wrapped cheese slices, a
half-eaten loaf of toast bread that had turned a fungal green
and white, a half-empty jar of capers, and seven bottles of
that cheap Swiss supermarket white wine, cooking wine,
basically. I unscrewed the top, poured half a glass, and filled
it the rest of the way at the faucet.

"Hand it to me please. Thank you. Well, what do you regret?"

EUROTRASH

. . . .

The eye contact between me and a young blonde woman in Tibet in 1999 who had put her empty film canisters in a recycling bin, in the lobby of the Lhasa Holiday Inn. I had been on my way to Mt. Kailash in western Tibet, wanting to write a book in which a dim-witted interior designer ends up there after a number of tribulations in order to perform a symbolic exchange. That I hadn't spoken to this woman, back then, in Lhasa, I thought.

"That I haven't taken care of you enough."

"Yes, that's very true. You were never there for me."

The constant, boundless drunkenness in Berlin. The drunken stroking of Frank Schirrmacher's hair in the back room of an Italian restaurant, late one evening in 2005. Frank, who had arguably been a friend, but with whom I could never speak as one does with a friend, and whose head I had tried to caress, and the way he flinched, saying, *Please don't do that, Christian, I don't like that.*

"You've abandoned me here. All this suffering is your fault," she said. I squirmed ever so slightly on the silk sofa. She was of course not wrong, and yet she was.

The attempt, around the same time, plastered again, to wrestle the then German foreign minister, Joschka Fischer, to the

63

ground, which ended with his bodyguards wrestling me down, pressing my shoulders into the ground with their knees while issuing directives into their headsets, one of them with his pistol drawn, holding me in check. That was at a party thrown by my publishing house in Berlin. To this day I don't know what I was thinking or why I wanted to attack Fischer, and I also don't remember my publisher, Helge Malchow, intervening and shouting, *Joschka, for Christ's sake, the zip ties really aren't necessary.*

"What about you?"

"I regret nothing," she said. "Not a thing."

"You don't?"

"Oh, don't give me these syrupy looks. You always look like a wet dog when you come to visit me."

"Oh, Mama."

"If you think I look terrible, just look at yourself in the mirror."

I noticed as I always did, as I had known for years, that the conversation simply couldn't be directed or shifted to something positive; it was a constant losing, a constant loss, a constant capitulation. She sat in her apartment like Miss Havisham, caught in a spider web of resentment, fury, and loneliness. In that moment I knew that either it would all continue on like this until her death or that now, only now, at this very second, I could break out of the cycle of abuse, out of the great wheel of fire, out of the spinning swastika.

And I said to her, Mama, with the emphasis on the second
a, Mama, we're going to go on a trip now together, the two
of us, and I rushed upstairs, up the spiral staircase she hadn't
set foot on in years, to pack her things. I grabbed two of her
beige overnight bags and tossed whatever inside: underwear,
sweaters, track pants, a skirt suit, two blazers, a silk scarf,
various blouses, loafers, and her Bulgari sunglasses, the
awful ones with the blue tinting.

Often, when old people who have lost touch would like to
suggest elegance, they resort to Bulgari. In my youth, there
had been a Bulgari glass case with Bulgari jewelry in the
dreadful discotheque Club Rotes Kliff on Sylt, in Kampen.
And in the dreadful luxury hotels in Marbella and Venice and
Positano there were always Bulgari grooming products lying
around in the bathrooms. Dreadful places like Qatar and
Dubai were serviced by dreadful luxury airlines who likewise offered Bulgari products in their in-flight shower stalls.
Over the years my mother had internalized the idea that Bulgari must embody something elegant, something desirable,
while in reality these products and this name only triggered
depression and thoughts of suicide. In which wardrobe were
her cashmere sweaters, please, I called down the stairs.

"Cashmere! Even in the greatest decrepitude we maintain
our poise!" she shouted up. "Which sweaters do you mean?
The Ferragamos are all down here, in the corner cabinet!"

. . . .

She certainly did not want to go on a trip, she shouted upstairs, out of the question, I must be completely insane. She was raging down there, grumbling and cursing and mumbling unintelligible things, and I heard her hobble into the kitchen to pour herself another glass of wine from the refrigerator. That pneumatic sucking sound from pulling on the refrigerator door, the sounds of the brief, intense burbling in the glass, of setting the bottle on the shelf, of the first, voracious gulp, then the second one, slower and more appreciative: from my earliest childhood they were so very familiar, as though these sounds had always been a part of me.

I came back down the stairs with her things packed, and as she watched I took three vodka bottles out of the freezer and carefully laid them into one of the bags, along with her medicine pouch with its various psychopharmaceuticals and a large travel kit with makeup, shampoo, soap, toothbrush, and cotton balls, and oddly enough she realized that she had no other choice, or rather she simply acquiesced, and then she asked, with some trepidation, when we would be leaving.

I said, right now, we're doing it now, it makes no sense to wait. It is the first step. *In girum imus nocte et consumimur igni.* Either we would always continue spinning around in the night, consumed by the fire, or we would leave, right now.

"Are we traveling to Africa?" she asked with mild concern in her voice. "Then we'll have to go to the bank first, though."

. . . .

"Where is your passport?"

"Oh, Africa! I have always loved the striped behinds of the zebras. At the Ngorongoro crater."

"Yes."

"Just a second. One for the road." She emptied her glass.

I phoned for a taxi, and she quickly gulped down another glass of that awful white wine. I took her arm, locked the apartment door from the outside, and on the way down the stairs to the exit we also grabbed her walker, and an umbrella. Then we were standing outside on the street, in autumn.

IV.

"Come on, tell me a story."

"Truth or fiction?"

"It doesn't matter to me. You decide."

"Okay. The story takes place here, right under our noses. There, uh, there had been a little shift to the right, and then another one, and then, six months later, an even bigger one. And the *Neue Zürcher Zeitung* and the *Weltwoche* and *Blick* and the *Schweizer Illustrierte* and the *Nebelspalter* and *Annabelle* had become the mouthpieces of the ruling party, whose members had started wearing little white Swiss crosses atop a red badge on their lapels."

"Oh."

"Yeah, and then the construction of new mosques was prohibited . . ."

". . . which isn't really so wrong actually, because come to think of it how many Christian churches are there in Saudi Arabia? Or in Pakistan for that matter?"

"Please just listen to me, Mama. German dentists and surgeons were deported one and all, as profiteers of the economic crisis. Then they'd begun administering Swiss German dialect exams and resettling the Tamils and the Tibetans to the

Mittelland or Oberland, into their own neighborhoods, as they were called. And then they came for the vegans."

"Why the vegans of all people?"

"And the police were armed and treated as equal to the military. And suddenly they were wearing red armbands with the white Swiss cross. Armored cars were parked at intersections; it was all happening quite stealthily but still completely out in the open, because it was the will of the people that these sorts of things were taking place."

"Oh please. You're nuts."

"Do you want to hear the story or not?"

"Pardon me. Go on."

"The Green Party was merged with the ruling party, the SVP. And the members of the Swiss People's Party were suddenly and overnight calling themselves the SNPS, the Swiss National People's Socialists, and the Greens and the Socialists started using that name then, too. And they saluted with the *Rütlischwur*, raising their thumb and first two fingers up high."

"This doesn't make any sense."

"Treaties with the European Union were annulled, as was the Schengen Agreement, and the Swiss borders were reinforced with tens of thousands of kilometers of new rolls of barbed wire. Cultural and economic relationships with Norway and Great Britain were strengthened, while the ones with Luxembourg and Poland and Tunisia languished. The domestic weapons industry was advanced and then a medium-sized scandal in the press was caused by claiming that Greek and Portuguese Communists had sold the Israelis over three hundred thousand live human organs."

"Oh my."

"Yeah, and the health food stores and Coop and Migros supermarkets were ordered not to carry tofu on their grocery shelves anymore, just Swiss cheeses and Swiss meats and sausage products, eggs, and rustic sourdough bread. Vegetarian spreads vanished from the aisles, as did soy milk and cashew patties. Armored cars took up position in front of the health food stores, like on Kreuzplatz in Zurich, to guarantee that they continued to sell exclusively animal products."

"And then?"

"Then they offered Swiss passports to healthy Belorussian, Albanian, and Korean men, provided they first pledged to learn Swiss German for a year and a half in immigration camps, for ten hours a day, and then to work in freedom for three years as mountain farmers, making cheese and tending livestock in the meadows, with a liege woman by their side who had to bear them at least three children."

"No!"

"Yes. That's exactly what it was like. Then they were given their Swiss passports and a guaranteed job as a taxi driver in Zurich, Geneva, Bern, or Basel, not in Subarus or anything, but in Mercedes or Teslas, metallic black, leather seats, wood veneer, fully automatic, a hundred eighty-four francs per hour minimum wage. And they spoke our Swiss German better than we do. They spoke it perfectly. And if they weren't yet wearing the little Swiss cross on their lapel, then they didn't need to be told to please pin it on; oh no, they did it gladly."

"That doesn't sound anything like the Switzerland I know."

"And at some point, Mama, it was in spring, and the crocuses had appeared everywhere, yellow and lush and beautiful, the prohibition on the death penalty was repealed, and from late that summer there were executions in Switzerland."

"You're telling it as if it were true."

"First, a flicker went over the land. The old people thought it wasn't right, and they were ashamed. This wasn't Swiss, they said, but the young people were indifferent. Why, do you think?"

"*Panem et . . . circenses.*"

"Exactly, very good, Mama. Pretty much. Then, bit by bit, they became part of everyday life, the executions. We felt that it would always affect someone else and not us, not the real Swiss, but only the Tamils and then maybe one day the Germans and *maybe* the vegans."

"Yeah."

"You and I weren't targeted, shadows that we were, and neither were the people who labored in the health food stores, and neither were the farmers. And the older folks who'd felt ill at ease with it all grew even older and ultimately got dementia, and after several years no one remembered what it had been like before the executions. They'd always carried them out hidden and in secret, except for traitors to the country. These, however, were pushed off bridges with a rope around their neck and weights in their pockets. From the Lorraine Bridge in Bern and the Münsterbrücke in Zurich. And although at first it seemed shocking and disgusting and un-Swiss of course, we not only had gotten used to these scenes in Lausanne and in Basel and in Chur, which were broadcast on Swiss national television, but in some respects had begun to accept them—and almost even to long for them, much as your father in Germany longed for the evening news every night."

"That is a dreadful story, Christian."

And then the taxi arrived. I saw her racially profile the driver quickly and quite automatically, and we got in, which of course took somewhat longer because of the walker. So I shall go on a trip with her, I'd thought, and maybe it will be her last.

She said we'd first head to the private bank downtown, the one behind the Hotel Baur au Lac. When the car set off, she leaned over to me and whispered in a conspiratorial tone that during the last financial crisis she'd bought shares, counterintuitively and quite successfully, in floor-cleaning machines and now had perhaps thirteen or fourteen million francs, primarily invested in German weapons systems and

Swiss dairy farms, specifically in shares of the companies
Rheinmetall and Emmi.

"That much money?"
  "Just imagine."
  "I always thought we were broke."
  "You're broke. Not me."
  "Why in the world would you have weapons shares?"
  "You know, I've often wondered that myself."

Lake Zurich to our left once again looked quite excruciatingly
exquisite because the autumn sun in particular and a *foehn*
wind sweeping down from the Alps made everything on the
lake appear razor-sharp and alluring. Little white sailboats
bobbled there, a whitewashed steamship glided through the
image, the Swiss flag fluttering merrily from its stern. It was
quite wonderful to ride in a taxi with my mother. We hadn't
done that together for who knows how long.

At the bank, though, they initially wouldn't even let us in.
I mean, how did this look: an old, half-drunk woman with
bruises and greasy hair and bloodshot eyes clinging to her
walker and heaving herself out of the elevator, her shadow of
a son, and a couple of battered travel bags?

I told her: she should just show her passport, she did have a
large account with them, she should feel no need to be embarrassed or shy. And indeed the bank clerk at the counter, after

first availing himself of an arrogance only Zurichers can pull off, was at once very courteous and polite, asking whether madame would like a coffee and that sort of thing while he flipped through her papers and did not further scrutinize my mother for her absent trappings of the bourgeoisie. Annoyed, I said no, no coffee, young man; my mother requires six hundred francs in cash, please. That would surely be enough for Africa, I said to my mother, after all I still had my credit cards. She looked at me, smiled, and said to the teller, no, no, sir, she would like six hundred thousand francs.

The fellow at the counter tugged at the diamond stud in his ear and without flinching asked whether she'd like six hundred one-thousand-franc bills, and all of a sudden I recalled my time with the billionaire Gustav Delbanco, whom I had met multiple times at the Hotel Savoy in London with my father. Delbanco had lugged around his money and his toothbrush in several Woolworth plastic bags, and he had smelled of garbage and feces. At the time, my father had brokered an oil painting for him, *The Fall of Man*, which later turned out to be a Rubens, which he, Delbanco, in turn swapped for *The Fall of Phaeton*, and then later hung over his fireplace in Sussex.

My mother now asked which portion of her money was invested in weapons technologies, and after two, three glances at the computer screen, the counter clerk printed her out a colorful pie chart. She picked up the piece of paper, gazed at it for a long while, and handed it to me. One half of the diagram, in blue, consisted of Rheinmetall shares, the other half, in red, of shares in Emmi.

"Please arrange for all the weapons shares to be converted into cash. Those blue ones there, I mean," she said. "We'll always need cash where we're going, my son and I. And would you please call us a taxi?"

"Yes, madame," the bank clerk said.

"Do you have a what's it called, a plastic bag?"

The man handed her a bag, and she dumped the bundle of six hundred one-thousand-franc bills into it. That had surely been what it was like with Gustav Delbanco, too. The thought would never have occurred to anyone that this man, who looked and smelled like a homeless person, was carrying around millions in a plastic bag. I thought about the fact that there was indeed a correlation between money and garbage, and as we walked toward the elevator, I told her so.

"I've known that for a very long time," she replied.

"It's exactly the same thing."

"You think I'm a stupid, heartless old woman. Just wait. We're going to give this money away."

"You mean donate it."

"No, no, really give it away, get rid of it, squander it. To whomever, randomly. And you're going to help me do it."

"Me?"

"Yes, you. Who else?"

What on earth had gotten into my mother? We reached the elevator and rode down, and I was taken aback and yet excited by this idea. My mother inspected herself in the double mirror and arranged her hair. She wet her thumb and wiped an imaginary stain off my cheek, and I let it happen despite having always hated when she did that, and then we stepped out onto the street and got into the taxi. The driver was politely holding the car door open for her, which I thought was the least he could do. He packed the walker into the trunk, and the traveling bags, too, and I unfolded the faded brochure of the commune from the pocket of my jacket, looked at the address written there, and told him he ought to please turn off the fare meter and drive us up to the Alps, to the Bernese Oberland, to Saanen.

"Exactly," said my mother. "And we'll give you a thousand francs. Oh, what the hell. Make it two thousand."

V.

Since my accident as a small child I had always been afraid
my throat might be slit. For decades I harbored this fear.
No one was ever allowed to touch my throat: not anywhere.
Sharp knives, the sight of straight razors in particular, made
me extremely queasy, and I'd get nauseated if one was close
by. This was not some overweening sensitivity, but naked
dread, a deeply affecting panic in the face of the thin, sharp,
lightning keenness of the blade. Even scratching or cutting
my finger on the edge of paper was a hideous thought, but the
arteries had to be protected; no one was allowed to get near
me, no one got to touch my throat, ever. It was like the stray
dog that had been beaten with an iron rod as a whelp and had
now internalized that proximity to humans could only entail
bad things.

As a small child, I'd been running through the woods
behind our chalet holding a bottle of fermented unfiltered
apple juice in my hands. The bottle had had a flip-top closure.
Apple juice, which I had intended to take to the child next
door, Rölfi, a farm boy of whom I was not particularly fond.
And I'd tripped over a root or something and had dropped
the bottle, which shattered on the ground. And then I myself

fell forward hands first onto the shards, one of which bored into the artery on my wrist. I ran home, and blood pumped in a thin squirt onto the forest floor. I had a clear view of that red cable of blood sputtering from my wrist, to the cadence of my body's heartbeat, onto the pine needles, onto the dark forest path, and then onto the lighter gravel.

After I'd arrived at the chalet—my parents were out of town—the completely overwhelmed nanny put me into the bathtub and held my wrist under the hot water, which naturally made everything much worse, until, only once my child-blood was sprayed all over the wall and slashed across the mirrors and onto the Chinese silk rugs, she finally thought she had better call an ambulance so they could stitch up my wrist at the hospital in Saanen where I had been born. I've recently seen the film *Caché* by Haneke—and now I'm getting to the point—there's of course this finale with the razor blade. I'd found it so excruciating that I thought I was going to die, truly.

Elsie von Oehrli would have known right away what had to be done with this bleeding child, but she had quit in order to marry a man over in the canton of Jura named Roger Voirol. I'd been horribly jealous, and my mother had hired another nanny, a young girl from Styria. She of course didn't have a clue, secretly smoked cigarettes in her *chambre de bonne*, and had frightened away our cat with her apathetic manner—she couldn't be bothered to do anything about anything.

Elsie von Oehrli wouldn't have held my wrist under the

hot stream of water in the tub, she wouldn't have let the fountains of blood sprayed throughout the chalet get to her, she would have known what to do. A tourniquet made of a kitchen towel torn into strips, for instance, then into a taxi, and straight down into the village to Dr. Sollberger, whose manly bearing, expressed through white corduroy trousers and a tweed blazer and bifocals, would have made everything all right again.

I looked out the window of the taxi. The tedious Zurich Mittelland was drawing past—the Lenzburg marmelade factory, then the blameless city of Olten—and imperceptibly, very slowly, the canton of Bern began: my home. In Bern, coming from Zurich, I was always initially astonished at the crassness in the faces of the Bernese, at their rustic deviousness and their wily Swiss instinct toward hostility, at their slightly protruding lower jaws and the expectant expression in their gaze, at this constant careful expectancy and their ossified insistence on their own provinciality. Though I have to say I'd always preferred the Bernese a thousand times over the Zurichers and their affected, absolutely baseless pomposity.

Since the fifties, Switzerland's highways have been in a state of perpetual repair. There was always a lane closure somewhere, then some orange cones would be standing around, and there was a seemingly abandoned construction trailer and a concrete mixer no one had been using for years. Everything was always trucked there and then, under cover of night, relocated to another site in order to give the impression that work, or anything at all, was being done. Along the short little span of highway between Milchbuck Tunnel and Zurich Airport, for example, work had been carried out for forty-four years now, always the one lane first, then the other, and then the cones would be redeployed anew, and allegedly new excavations would take place and cordons would be re-erected and fresh concrete would be poured. It had been that way for decades, it had been that way for almost half a century.

And the food in Switzerland, which always tasted so much better than it did elsewhere? It was manufactured by child slaves who added drugs from the Nestlé company so that people enjoyed eating it and did as they were told and remained good Swiss. The Swiss would all eat their Soylent Green and go to work and go to sleep and wake up the following day, and absolutely nothing would happen. There was no music and no films and no literature; there was nothing whatsoever in Switzerland except that Swiss longing for more banal luxury, the desire for sushi and colorful sneakers and Porsche Cayennes and the construction of further gigantic home improvement centers in the sprawling *Agglos*.

I glanced sideways at my mother, asleep beside me in the backseat of the car. Her mouth was open ever so slightly. And I saw my mother who would always feign death on the laundry room floor of the chalet in Gstaad, when I was small. I'd felt unimaginable fear at the sight of her lying there on her back next to the washing machine, her mouth slightly open. I might have been perhaps five years old. I'd stuck my little fingers into her nose, tickled her side, tugged at her ear, stroked her hair—these had been my futile attempts to revive her. I'd started screaming, calling for my father in my terror and then, when he didn't show up, for the sorcerer figure in my puppet theater who wore a purple, star-bedecked cape and a black hat.

As a child I'd always felt that in pretending to be dead my mother desired retribution, a diffuse retribution, a kind of revenge for the misery incurred that she'd told me about on her eightieth birthday on the Winterthur psychiatric ward and which I'd suspected nothing about at the time. My childhood dreams almost resembled the final scene from the Dürrenmatt film adaptation *It Happened in Broad Daylight*, in which police detective Matthäi, played by Heinz Rühmann, shows little Annemarie a sock puppet, smiling, while his blood runs down his wrist. The child molester Gert Fröbe had slashed him with a razor blade in the forest while the detective was saving the little girl. He'd lured her into the woods with little chocolate hedgehogs. I've never learned why my mother, who once so adored eating chocolate hedgehogs, would often play dead when I was little. A Heinz Rühmann with a sock puppet on his hand had never appeared to her.

. . . .

The commune I was having us driven to was located in Saanen, where I was born, outside Gstaad. We drove through the narrow Simmen Valley, through the village of Zwei-simmen. This was where that peculiar antique dealer Ernst Nacht had had his warehouse, to which my father and I had come whenever he'd wanted to sell rustic lumber he'd fina-gled cheaply from high Alpine huts, with the date notched in. On these beams the years 1671, 1710, and 1730 were eas-ily legible. And Ernst Nacht, whose name and severe crew cut had always aroused uneasiness in me, had run his rough hands over the timber beams, inspecting what my father had towed in, and then had them carried down to his shady ware-house, here in the village called Zweisimmen. My father had stuck Herr Nacht's hundred-franc bills in the rear pocket of his white corduroy trousers and driven back with me to Gstaad in his pale blue VW Beetle with the ski rack on the roof. I became queasy with melancholy and forsaken child-hood and all that.

"I need to go," said my mother.

"Pee?"

"No, the other one."

"Then we'll stop at the next gas station."

"I mean I've already gone."

"How do you mean? In your trousers?"

"No, in the bag."

"Huh? What bag?"

"Here, in this one here. Feel."

"What in the world is that?"

"It's a stoma, a colostomy bag."

"Oh."

I didn't know she had a colostomy bag. It was an incursion into reality. I was confronted with something about which I hadn't the slightest clue; I didn't know anything like that existed outside of an issue of *Mad* magazine. And now my own mother had one.

"And what do we do now?"

"Now we have to stop somewhere. And then you will please change my bag."

"Okay."

"Usually the housekeeper does this."

"Wow, okay, she did that, too?"

"Yes, she was always a great help to me, unlike you."

"Monsieur, please pull off over here to the right, over there, and stop."

I carefully lifted up first her sweater and then her blouse from her abdomen. There actually was this bag connected to her that was gurgling very slightly.

. . . .

"I can't do this."

"Well, neither can I," she said.

The taxi driver looked into the rearview mirror. I fished out the pair of promised thousand-franc notes from my mother's plastic bag and passed them up front to the driver, and with a sheepish fanning motion of my hand indicated to him to look away. Then I reached back, opened one of the travel bags, took out a bottle of vodka, and opened it.

"Those tiny bottles they always give you on airplanes are much more practical," my mother said.

"Do you really not know how to do this? Surely you've watched before when they've been changed."

"No, I always look away, I can't stand to watch. Pass me the bottle."

"Don't you at least want to use a paper cup, from the gas station?"

"The things you worry about."

She drank one, two, finally three big gulps from the vodka bottle. The driver stared ahead inexorably, having pocketed the thousand-franc bills. Outside it looked as though it might soon snow. I tried to buy a little time.

. . . .

"You're sure you don't have any . . . uh . . . replacement bags with you?"

"Oh, I do, I do, you did pack the makeup case, the big one with the Liberty pattern. There are bags in there. And plus you can buy them in any pharmacy."

"Do you need a needle for it?"

"What do you mean, a needle?"

"Well, a syringe."

"No, of course not."

"Can I suggest something, Mama?"

"Please do."

"We'll drive to a hotel now where I've made a reservation for us. It's not much farther at all. We'll check in there, and then I promise you I'll snap you on a new bag."

"Right. I don't want to carry around this full old thing with me for hours and hours."

I requested we drive on, and we drove on, up the mountain roads, to Schönried, and then back down the other side into the broad valley, so familiar to me, of the Saanenland. The wooden houses to the left and right lay low and squat; the snow load expected in the winter ahead seemed already now, in autumn, to strain the pointy pitched roofs. In the past the weather report on Swiss radio would always say *Tonight it will snow down into the bottomlands*, which had always greatly upset me as a child because I of course lived high up in the mountains. This mention of bottomlands, a word that evoked a world beyond and below my own, had always filled me with a premonition of terror, with the knowledge of impending calamity.

Now and again, by the side of the road, a wooden pole painted orangish red jutted out of the grassy embankment. The colostomy bag gurgled softly. I had tears in my eyes.

"What's wrong? Why are you sad?"

"I haven't been here since I was little. I've always loved the mountains so much."

"I've always hated them. They crushed me, for years, for decades. These narrow valleys, you can only see the sun in them at midday, otherwise everything is always in shadow the whole time. These frigid heights up there, the white sky, the glaciers, ten thousand years of ice. I hate them."

"So what did you love then?"

"I always wanted to go back to Africa. And now it's kind of too late, Christian, my boy."

"I love three things. I love a dream of love I once had, I love you, and I love this part of the earth here."

"And which one of these do you love most?"

"The dream."

We drove through the sun-draped valley of my childhood, and when we stopped in front of the commune, she sorted and arranged her hair, and put on her sunglasses.

. . . .

"Listen. That thing with the dream, what you just said."

"Yeah."

"That's not by you, Christian. You're bluffing. I know you. You read that in . . . wait . . . in . . . it's on the tip of my tongue. In Knut Hamsun."

"What did you say?"

VI.

I'd planned to trick my mother into believing the commune's dilapidated chalet was that fine hotel in which I'd made us a reservation. I didn't even feel bad for wanting to deceive her—on the contrary. Perhaps we might begin by giving away her money right here and now. A vegetarian commune like this one might be able to use our family's filthy Swiss francs in a meaningful way. Perhaps they needed new windows, or a new roof, or they might buy an enormous herd of sheep with it or something.

We got out, the taxi driver carried our luggage to the door and waited to see whether yet another gratuity might be forthcoming, but I never give tips as a matter of principle, a trait I have from my mother, who also gives zero tips.

My father the windbag, on the other hand, had always carried in his right palm a twenty-franc note folded up into a little square so that he might conspiratorially pass it to servants while shaking hands. After his death, I'd tried out this patronizing gesture a few times. With pinky and ring finger, the waiter or hotelier would receive the dainty paper cushion and slip it into his own pocket, quite by reflex. Only after the guest had been seen off could the waiter determine whether the crinkled bill was a hundred-franc note or merely a single dollar.

My father had always thought people would remember him well if he left a generous tip everywhere and at all times, but I never believed him. The launch captain on the river Elbe for sure did not remember him either, or those two hundred euros, or the plastic bag with my father's ashes, tossed into the grayish, murky river near Hamburg.

It seemed the large, rustic, run-down chalet before which my mother and I were now standing was merely the commune's guesthouse. The commune itself was situated high up in an Alpine meadow between the two mountains Eggli and La Videmanette, but no one was up there now because in autumn you couldn't make it up or back down due to snow.

So the commune only ran in summer. Sheep shearing and apple picking and what have you was done in autumn, though the woolen sweaters and blankets and scarves and the like were knitted in winter, seated by the fire, here in the guesthouse. I'd reflected on this the previous night, in my hotel room in Zurich, while staring at the ceiling, sleepless, beset by memories.

The taxi drove off, leaving behind a small, quickly dissipating cloud of exhaust at our knees. I took my mother by the arm. Gingerly we walked along the gravel of the chalet's drive toward the entrance. It was almost cold. She said she didn't need her walker, and where in the world were the suitcase carriers at this establishment? Gstaad must have changed quite a bit since the last time she had been here, forty years ago, and I replied that this was Saanen, right next to Gstaad, seeing that you couldn't stay in Gstaad anymore because of all the Prada boutiques. I deposited her at the door to the guesthouse, told her to please wait for a moment, and ran back to fetch the overnight bags and her walker.

Over in Gstaad the native population was sitting on real estate worth so extravagantly much that even parcels in the middle of Tokyo and London would appear inexpensive by comparison. Thousands of huge chalets had sprung up here in the Saanenland, all constructed in the exact same style. According to the prescribed design, there had to be two balconies on the front, then pitched roofs, low-hanging eaves, and the whole thing was to be fashioned inside and outside from unsightly blond wood that would darken handsomely over the years. And a peculiar kind of people had sprung up here in the last sixty years: essentially coarse, aloof mountain farmers whose minute plots of land were suddenly worth hundreds of millions of francs, and these fantastic prices depended on which oligarchs showed up to ski in that particular season. It had become a valley of absurdities, my homeland. This entire Debordian spectacle had naturally also extended to the neighboring village of Saanen, even out to Feutersoey, Rougemont, and Château-d'Œx.

No one came to the door. I suppose I had expected a young woman, who'd be wearing round steel glasses and the same scratchy woolen wares I'd seen the previous evening at the stall in Zurich, or maybe a bearded man with honest and kind eyes. We buzzed, waited a while, and when still no one appeared, we went inside, glad to escape the brisk autumn air. My mother seemed a bit confused, but quite content to get to be in a hotel lobby finally. She had not set foot in a hotel in seven or more years, having seen the insides of various mental institutions only, and of course of all hospitals and clinics in Zurich.

The fairly insignificant foyer featured only a couple of wing chairs upholstered in yellow corduroy, a tatty shag carpet, a pot with a red poinsettia, a few floor lamps of indeterminate age, and a large, almost empty bookshelf with some packets of tea stacked atop books by Richard Coudenhove-Kalergi and Richard Bach. Balthus's Grand Chalet it was not. A wall clock ticked softly. The whole place smelled of damp laundry. I felt the room had been lost to time in a very welcoming way; the last forty-five, fifty years hadn't taken place here. My mother removed the book *Jonathan Livingston Seagull* from the shelf, leafed through it for a bit, and set it aside again.

"Where are all the staff?" she whispered.

"I don't know, Mama. I hope that they have a room for us."

"Well, I would not pay too much for this hotel. Did you see? There's dust everywhere and god knows what else. And then these rugs."

"Maybe . . . maybe we could give them some money so they could do a proper renovation."

"That's a fantastic idea."

"How do a couple hundred thousand francs sound?"

"But then we won't pay for the room."

"Okay."

Lying on a sideboard were several room keys, their small plastic pendants furnished with different names. I took one of them, lumbered down the hall, and my mother followed me, stooped over her walker. It felt good to be taking the initiative. I'd chosen the key inscribed *Nestor*, stopped outside the room with the corresponding nameplate, and unlocked it.

My mother removed her quilted jacket, sat down on the bed, pushed up her blouse from her abdomen, looked at me, and exhaled. The room was decorated in faded striped wallpaper. A bleak hill could be seen outside the window, as well as some branches. I unzipped one of the travel bags and, from her toiletry kit, took a flesh-colored pouch with a kind of adhesive ring attached to the front. I reached very carefully for the full bag hanging at her belly and twisted the little valve. It disengaged very easily, and I took the fresh rubber sack and gently screwed it onto the exposed thing on her belly until something on it snapped into place. My mother smiled. I smiled. I had the pleasurable feeling of having made amends for something. I took her hand.

She wanted to lie down for a bit now, she said, and no

sooner than she'd put her feet up and her head on the pillow, she was already asleep. So I set the opened vodka bottle on the night table for her, drew a heart and *Be right back* on a yellow Post-It note, laid two phenobarbital tablets next to it, and went to the foyer to find someone. Somebody had to be working or living here. You couldn't just leave a whole chalet unlocked like this.

In any case, before we gave away the two or three hundred thousand francs, I wanted to know a little more about this commune. I had a definite feeling of uneasiness, which I guess was fueled by various horror films. And there was in fact now an older blond man standing in the rear of the foyer, over by the bookshelf, who was looking at me. He was leaning his elbow against the windowsill while rolling a cigarette and licking the tiny rubberized strip with the tip of his tongue. He was wearing jeans and hiking boots, a checkered lumberjack shirt, and a wool vest over it.

I cleared my throat and said my mother and I were sorry to have just come inside like this, at which he grinned and said it was more than fine, we were most welcome, and where had we heard about the Dirk Hamer Commune? I said I'd bought a wool sweater at a stand in Zurich, just yesterday, where they'd given me a brochure. Uh-huh, he responded, while wiping a crumb of tobacco from his lower lip with his thumb. His teeth were yellowed and ugly.

The chalet was empty and unoccupied in the fall, so he was glad of our visit. He was something like the German steward of the guesthouse. Was I perhaps a vegetarian? And, he had to say, I did somehow look familiar to him. Was I not perhaps a writer? Wasn't I the author of *Measuring the World*?

I said yes, yes, and told him I was so pleased he had read it. So the commune was named after Dirk Hamer. And who was this Hamer, I asked. The man now lit the hand-rolled cigarette and came closer while explaining to me that Dirk Hamer was the son of their leader, who had been shot and killed by Prince Vittorio Emanuele of Savoy, on his yacht, while anchored off Corsica.

The founder of this place, Ryke Geerd Hamer, Dirk's father, had realized that each and every illness was triggered by something called a conflict shock, which meant that every illness had to be understood as a biological scheme of nature created to resolve an unexpected biological conflict. I must admit that from that point on I kind of stopped listening; it all seemed really abstruse to me. The man, who was actually quite friendly though also intensely repulsive, then said something about a New Germanic Medicine that Hamer senior had developed, and that this alone would be able to create the coming race, that's what they were all working toward together here, toward stopping cancer, in the Germanic way. He smiled with his yellow teeth. At that moment I decided that we would not give the money to this person and this commune under any circumstances.

Basically, my mother and I would need to decamp from this place immediately. The whole situation here was really skirting the edge of the abnormal. I thanked him somewhat sanctimoniously, it seemed to me, and walked back toward the room, at which the man called after me, see you soon, supper would be in a bit, around seven, over in the small dining room. Yes, thanks, great, I just had to fetch my mother, I replied.

While I was away, my mother had of course eaten both phenobarbital tablets, and the vodka bottle was half empty. Good god. I switched on the light, took her hand, and gently shook her arm. She opened her eyes, which were rolled back, and her eyelids fluttered uncontrollably. Why hadn't I read the phenobarbital instructions? Normally a tablet should contain what, thirty or at most eighty milligrams? With my mother's years of consumption, wouldn't she have built up some sort of resistance? I shouted two, three times whether she was awake, while fumbling with the package. The pills were two hundred milligrams each, and she had taken two of them, washing them down with the vodka.

They were these thingies with a kink in the middle which you were only ever supposed to take at most half of. Oh god. Oh god. I quickly went and got a towel from the bathroom and an orange plastic toothbrush cup full of water and began wiping her forehead with the dampened terry cloth. I was such an idiot. What unbelievable stupidity. I'd gone and actually poisoned her. Her eyes were shut again. It seemed she was much paler than normal, but this could also have been the crummy lighting in the room. I kept daubing with the towel, pinching her earlobes, stroking her greasy hair. There was no reaction. A very small bubble of saliva rose between her lips.

"Mama, wake up! This can't be happening. Mama! We'll go to the hairdresser, you know. If you wake back up now, then we'll go, you and me, and we'll have your hair done nicely, maybe even much shorter, would you like that? Mama?"

I felt I'd only ever spouted platitudes my whole life long. No, I *knew* I'd only ever spouted platitudes my whole life long. Never had anything I'd ever said been relevant in any way, never could what I said compete with what was inside me.

"I was always most afraid of guests coming into our house and smirking at us, you know, because we were unable to make amusing conversation at dinner. Papa wasn't able to either. Surely you must remember that. He was completely autistic when people came over, I got that from him."

She wasn't moving at all. She'd always been happiest when she'd been listening to stories. I couldn't think of a story no matter how hard I tried. Please, any story at all.

"Mama, listen, do you know the story of Mary Watson? Don't you want to hear it? Okay, so, uh . . . Mary Watson had been drifting in the sea for eight days and around forty miles with her four-month-old baby named, uh . . . Ferrier and of course Ah Sam, her horribly wounded Chinese servant. In an iron ship's cistern, cut in half, that had once been used to boil . . . sea cucumbers. Mama? This after Aborigines from the mainland had attacked the Bêche-de-Mer station of her absent husband on, uh . . . Lizard Island. Her diary describing her last days was found with her remains in 1882. Can you hear me?"

She didn't react. This couldn't be happening. Her story wasn't over, damn it, most certainly not in this bedroom of a dingy Nazi commune in Switzerland. I took both her hands in mine.

"Mama! Listen! Mary Watson and her husband had established their sea cucumber station near a small spring, the only freshwater supply on the island. Mary had also accidentally set foot . . . on an indigenous ceremonial site that was normally taboo for women and children."

Was she still breathing? I couldn't tell. I squeezed and kneaded her hands until they turned red and purple.

"The Aborigines attacked Ah Sam, who suffered seven awful spear wounds. Another servant, uh . . . he was called Ah Leung . . . he was killed in their vegetable garden, which he'd lovingly tended. Mary Watson initially frightened off the Aborigines by firing her revolver, and then they put out to sea inside this iron tub, in the hope of being picked up by a passing ship. Mary and her baby and Ah Sam drifted for, uh . . . for about a week, and they occasionally came ashore on reefs and small islands. Mary Watson's last diary entry ended with *No water. Almost dead with thirst.*"

"How come they hadn't taken any water with them? Everybody knows you have to take water with you no matter where you're going."

"My god, there you are."

"I always carry water with me, always."

"Mama."

"How does the story end?"

"You were pretending to be dead."

"Yes."

"Like you used to."

"Like I used to."

"I was so horribly worried."

"Nonsense. That was just your sense of guilt. I'm not going to die. Now how does this story end?"

"Well, the remains of Mary and her baby were found a few weeks later in the mangroves on Howick Island, lying in their iron cistern, covered by fresh rainwater after a tropical downpour. Ah Sam had died on the beach nearby. There was a hidden freshwater spring, also nearby, that they hadn't found."

"That's very sad, the thing about the tropical downpour."

"Isn't it?"

"That's a very good story."

. . . .

She pulled herself together, we arranged her hair, and she put on a white turtleneck sweater, a skirt suit on top, and a pair of slippers on her sleep-swollen feet. She draped a simple string of pearls around her neck, and then we went to dinner, slowly, she without her walker.

In the breakfast room a little table had been set for us with a blue-checkered paper tablecloth on it as well as white plates, glasses, and paper napkins for each of us. A candle had been lit, which made my mother quite happy.

A somewhat rotund Bernese Oberland woman in an apron with Snoopy and Woodstock on the front brought dishes from the kitchen and set them on the table. It was a beef goulash with potatoes, along with a green salad dressed with several flesh-colored strips of ham. It wasn't vegetarian here at all, quite the contrary.

"I haven't yet introduced myself," said the blond man from before as he came in. He'd since combed his sparse hair straight back with water and was now wearing a shawl of deep red velvet, an Indian bindi on his forehead, and those jeans and hiking boots.

"I, too, am seeing you for the first time," said my mother.

"May I join you?"

"Please do. Apologies, I'm still a bit disheveled from my afternoon nap."

"Not a problem, madame. I'd spoken with your son earlier and explained to him the principles of our leader."

"Yes, of course. The owner surely hails from an ancient dynasty of Swiss hoteliers."

This was all more than unpleasant for me. My mother could not under any circumstances learn that this was not a hotel. Just then, I remembered the Hotel Baur au Lac in Zurich. Once, when I was perhaps twenty, I'd had dinner there one evening with my father. He was wearing his dove gray suit from Davies and Son and the very narrow red-and-blue-striped, fake regimental tie. And when the waiters hadn't shown him the respect and reverence he felt he was due and he had sent for the bill, he wrote KRACHT on it in very large capital letters at the bottom. His name was also by chance the name of the hotel's owner (no relation), which he had hoped would send an awestruck shiver through the waitstaff, and that upon exiting the hotel's revolving door he could buy even more servility with the twenty-franc bill cleverly folded in his hand. Silly man.

"Times are hard, madame. We don't have as many visitors as we did ten years ago. Monsieur Ryke Geerd Hamer has, how should I put it, fallen slightly out of favor."

"Oh yes. The Hamers," my mother said. "I know them well. An old hotel dynasty. Hard times. Now, we thought, my son and I, we wanted perhaps to give you some money if you're doing so poorly."

"Thank you kindly. But that is really not necessary," the man replied. "How much were you thinking?"

"Let me see. We withdrew six hundred francs from the bank. Two thousand we gave to the taxi driver. Or did we give him six hundred thousand? No, that can't be right. I've gotten so bad at math. I hate old age. Oh, I detest it. Well, what do you say?" She looked at me.

"Uh."

"I actually wanted to come in my Mercedes, but it's in storage. My son here hides the car key from me, thinking I can't drive anymore."

"Well," the man said, "it certainly is more pleasant when someone else does the driving." I considered for an instant whether I ought to tell her, here and now, that her Mercedes was gone forever in Eastern Europe, stolen by her housekeeper and shipped to Macedonia. No, better not.

"Do you have the money here with you?" he asked.

"But of course we do. Don't we, Christian?"

"Christian?" The man furrowed his brow. "Your name isn't Daniel? I can't believe it. You're not Daniel Kehlmann?"

"And you? Your commune isn't vegetarian either?"

Feeble wit on my part. Usually ripostes only occurred to me hours later, when it was too late. Somehow I now had to manage this whole thing better, I thought; it could not keep on going like this, I had to bring the conversation under my control, and so I skewered a potato onto my fork.

. . . .

"Do you know what Adorno said about vegetarianism?"

"No," the man said.

"Auschwitz begins in the slaughterhouse."

"Christian. Is this really necessary now?"

"I would prefer, Mama, that you not comment on this. Not you, nor your family either."

"You mean because your grandfather was a Nazi."

"And what a perfect Nazi he was. The most loyal of all. Until his very last breath."

"Let me finish . . ."

". . . No. You let me finish, please. You don't have the slightest clue about any of this. You have no right to express an opinion. You don't realize or don't want to realize that your father refused to accept any part of his guilt, just as you also refuse to accept it, your guilt and his."

"I was seven when the war ended."

"But you were old enough later to tell your father that he was a criminal."

"No. I couldn't do that. But that's the reason I then married your father," she said, brushing her hair into place. "Why would you want to confront me with all this stuff now, now, when I'm way past eighty?"

"Excuse me, may I say something?"

"No, young man, you may not. Most certainly not. Not you. My husband was a Social Democrat, his whole life long. Are you aware of what Martin Walser said? Our entire society constructed Auschwitz. Can you conceive of that? Do you know what is meant by that?"

"Uh . . ."

"Have you ever seen anything of the unbridled cruelty of people?"

"Well, I . . ."

"I think not. So shut up. And now you're attacking my son, for not being called Daniel? Daniel? The very nerve."

"Thank you, Mama."

"Your gratitude comes a bit late, but better than not at all."

"Then I guess I'll be going now." He smiled at us, and it was not at all meant nicely. It was a malicious smile, a horrid smile. He resembled an unshaven, yellow-toothed vampire. Actually, no, he was looking at us as if we were already strangled cats in a plastic noose.

"Sleep well, mother and son. For sleep is a rose, as the Russians say."

"*Et rose elle a vécu ce que vivent les roses, l'espace d'un matin*," she replied, and *boom*, there it was, her second favorite quote. It was from Malherbe, and again it was perfect. My mother sure knew her French writers.

"And by the way," she yelled after him, "your goulash tastes like it's from a can." This wasn't like my mother at all. Traveling very obviously became her, I thought. Perhaps we really should go to Africa after all.

VII.

We slept in our shared room although I did not sleep, my mother's snoring gentle and fluttering. Nocturnal thoughts popped up incessantly, those spinning thoughts, a circling of the flame amid the darkness. I was sitting aboard a plane. I was lying in bed, which was a plane. Which river was that down below? Why did I like the name of the city Lahore so very much? There lay the Indus Valley, there the Sind Valley, there the Hindu Kush, Hindu-Killer. I could not sleep. I also could not really tolerate overt aggression very well. I had never seen my mother like that. I had always seen my mother just like that. The Hindu Kush. Perhaps I had also just simply never seen her. The Pamir Mountains, and Nanga Parbat. In the early 1960s, my mother had studied French, stenography, and etiquette as well as a bit of literature in Montreux.

What had it been like back then? Why did I harbor such a longing for this time, for silk-lined suits in polyester and wool? For the curvature of black mudguards, for the sans serif font of train station signage? For gentlemen smoking cigarettes while carrying umbrellas, for their flannel sleeves in light gray and the immaculate white of their dress shirts beneath? That intense desire for narrow ties, for the triangular folds of handkerchiefs protruding from the breast pockets of blazers, for spectacles made of Bakelite.

These men had read the newspaper while waiting for their engagements in Switzerland's tearooms, in those forever bygone institutions of Calvinism. You did not go to bars or pubs in those days; you went to a tearoom in the evening, to drink tea with milk and sugar. Had my mother visited those tearooms, in Montreux, in the early sixties? Had she met young men her age there who paid her compliments behind their upraised teacups in the nightingalish singsong of Swiss French? Had they had curly hair, green eyes, a genial complexion, a thin mustache like David Niven, my potential fathers who never became my father?

Sleep, please come, I thought, at three thirty. Perhaps I should take one of my mother's phenobarbital tablets. No, it was entirely out of the question for me to do that. Then I would be like her. How sad, I thought, that this commune I had looked forward to had turned out to be a bunch of Nazi fraudsters. I had wanted to meet good people and give them the contaminated money we had swindled from arms factories. And my mother, who was not in her right mind, had realized not only that these were not the right people, but the phoniest of the phony, and had put a stop to it. Where did this certainty in her come from?

I was lying on my back in bed, still wearing my clothes and shoes, unwashed like the billionaire Gustav Delbanco. I had stuffed the plastic bag with the money under my pillow.

And I suddenly realized that I had always, all my life, put everything under the bed. I would stow the cheese sandwiches sneaked from the kitchen at night under the bed, back when I met my wife, and then later I would put the bread knife and the ice pick beneath the bed, to defend my family, and the crowbars and the walking sticks with the pointy brass duck-bill grips and my beloved pig stick from Papua New Guinea.

And my father had stored his rolled-up Kirchners and Munchs and Swiss francs under his bed, and I had inherited this instinct from him, except in my case they had always been instruments for warding off danger. For my father it had been the simple desire never to have to be poor again, to feel as though he actually owned the things under his bed, items no one could ever take away from him because he was lying on top of them. And as I now saw him, he really had been a peculiar little man, short and wiry and slender with little hair, in those light gray suits, an evasive man who hid behind his bright blue eyes. He had always been an enigmatic person to me. He had been a repository of secrets, which only surfaced after his death.

Once one summer, he had rented for us in Cascais the home of the Portuguese banking family Espírito Santo, a magnificent villa on a spit of land with private access to the sea. He was walking with me from the home's entrance through a narrow alleyway toward the town center when a dented purple Renault tried to squeeze its way past. There was space between his knee and the front fender of the vehicle, which was rolling past him quite slowly, at least thirty centimeters between them, I would have thought. Yet my father screamed out and grabbed his shin, doubled over in pain as though the car had not just glanced him, but shattered his knee.

Worried, the driver got out of his vehicle to attempt to help my father, at which he, his face contorted in pain, ordered the driver to the house, only a few meters away, which of course belonged to one of the country's wealthiest and most influential families. There, in the salon, limping, he cast himself onto a Louis XVI ottoman, threw up his leg, and basked in reflecting that the poor driver of the R4 was dazzled in the face of so much elegance, influence, and power—and of course feeling as though he had made the worst mistake of his life—although nothing, truly nothing at all, had happened. My father had blown up the little incident merely to boast in front of some random Portuguese man off the street and humiliate him.

My father had loved power, and was able to create for himself an impenetrable carapace and the detachment he needed by tormenting and debasing others. And sometimes I wondered whether my entire family fed off the humiliation of others, whether they defined themselves through an elitism that was merely the air of a middle class wanting to ascend to the upper class, afraid of nothing more than its own proletarian background.

On the other hand, it was so terribly easy to see right through it all, this showing off, and had been since I was a young child. He must have seen that, my father. It had always been so very obvious. During our mostly silent breakfasts together at his château on Lake Geneva, he would always twist the soft insides of the bread rolls into balls, on the table, then stash these little remnants in his trouser pocket, before tossing them to the chickens in order to watch them fight over the scraps. It had been amusing, it had been petty, callow, and sad.

Had the German and Norwegian expressionists—into whose work caste and class had not really figured—perhaps put him in mind of a purplish dreamscape, beyond the bourgeois? Nolde, Munch, and Pechstein had always been his favorites, Kirchner and Heckel had always been his favorites, while the political artists George Grosz or Otto Dix had meant nothing to my father. Max Beckmann, on the other hand, had been an exception for him; he'd owned several etchings and paintings. Yet that dreamscape had only been attainable with money. Never had there been a spirituality attached to art. Mystical and elevated matters had remained alien to him; I hadn't even been baptized. There'd been no alternate world. For him there was only this world, and it had ended in the river Elbe in a plastic bag. A grave was not something he wanted, nor did he want a memorial stone, nor discussions, nor remembrance, and afterward there had been nothing but silence and extinction. And the paintings?

In the end, they had been sold off at Kornfeld and Sotheby's and Grisebach. Nothing grand had been left. Not a single one of his dreams. Now, once more, the fissured ice giants of the Hindu Kush appeared before me, and the phenobarbital package lying on the night table beside my sleeping mother.

Around four a.m. I heard faint footsteps out in the hallway. I was unsure whether I might not already have fallen asleep. With an electric twitch all over my skin, I jolted up, fully awake. The steps halted, in front of our door. Then, very quietly and tentatively, a key was inserted into the lock from the outside.

I leapt up and first braced my shoulder against the door, then removed my belt in a flash, tied the handle tightly, and hooked the buckle to a coat peg beside the door. Why hadn't I just locked it? Someone was trying to force the door from the outside, but the belt held. There was feeble, half-livid kicking, and I stood ready to seize the night table lamp a pace away and use it as a blunt instrument. Then I heard footsteps receding, and then once more the calm, velveteen rattling of my mother, who was lying supine, not moving.

At around six thirty, I sat up, rubbing my hands over my face and eyes while my mother, who as ever had long been awake, performed her morning ablutions. As she applied lipstick and rubbed some rouge over her scab-covered cheekbones, I told her we had to get out of here, as fast as possible in fact. Did she need another pouch first? Yes, she said, and I attended to that with much greater adroitness than even yesterday, and it no longer bothered me as much. I helped her to get dressed; she had selected a canary yellow skirt suit.

I had not thought her capable of that whole scene yesterday night. I mean, I knew myself and that I could react to physical danger, for instance, lightning fast and with teeth-baring snarls like a cornered animal, but I had never seen my mother like that. All of a sudden, she had a strength unknown to me to put up a fight, which was indeed astonishing, at over eighty. She had, after all, been forced to assert herself not only against the collective SS horror of her father all her life, but also against my father, her very wealthy husband.

The fundamental problem was always money, she had once told me, years earlier, when she'd gone to the psychiatric ward for the first time, then in Meiringen. Money is the instrument of oppression, don't forget that, my boy, she had said, that's how they get you, especially here in Switzerland. She had been sipping from a soft drink bottle secretly spiked with vodka in the reception area, and here she was. This country, Switzerland that is, didn't even exist until the English invented it at the end of the eighteenth century, she had said, until it was captured on postcards, as a panorama, as a sight, as a view.

She had herself committed at the Meiringen clinic, had written her name on the form at reception with a scratchy black marker while she turned to me, her sunglasses in her whitening hair, the receptionist handing her more clipboards to fill out and my mother impressing upon me that that's when the Swiss saw how easily money could be made from their pleasant vistas, which until then they hadn't found to be anything special, but if foreigners wanted to pay for them, why not.

The receptionist had looked at me and raised her eyebrows slightly and filed the signed pieces of paper attesting to my mother's self-committal into a cabinet, and then we said our goodbyes. She had been full of pluck, full of jaunty energy, on account of the vodka lemon soda, perhaps also on account of her committal, and I had called after her that she really ought to see the Reichenbach Falls if she had time, just behind and uphill from the clinic, and then she had vanished into the corridors of the institution, her Ferragamo handbag clutched tightly to her, and I had watched her go with a lump in my throat. Even then I had thought she was actually quite an extraordinary person. And if she hadn't been my mother, I had thought, I might have liked to meet her.

I spoke to her in the car on the way to the clinic that she should take care to eat properly in the dining hall or in her room. And she had said food was a matter of indifference to her—she also didn't go to farmers' markets in Zurich to buy vegetables or whatever. And I had told her that the market at Bürkliplatz, for instance, was a really fantastic place to get fresh organic fruit and cheese of all stripes and thick-crusted farmhouse bread, warm from the oven. And she had then

answered, my boy, she had said, it is the dubious privilege of
the petite bourgeoisie to have an interest in fruit and cheese
and fresh cauliflower, she refused to do so, she would eat
only ready-made meals, everything else was pedestrian, and
as far as she was concerned she could eat fish squares from
the supermarket freezer until the end of her days.

I packed our things into the bags, and we crept out of the
room called Nestor. No one prevented us from doing so,
despite the walker making a kind of jolting noise whenever
my mother pushed the thing over the hallway thresholds.
The house was devoid of people, and the linoleum floor dif-
fusely reflected our shadows. The creepy man from the night
before did not show himself, although now would be the time
to relieve us of the money bag. But nothing happened. He did
not appear, although as a precaution I had jammed my mother's house keys into my right hand, the sharp tips of each key
jutting out from between my fingers, like a small spiked mace
in my hand.

Outside we sensed the rising sun behind the mountains,
behind Eggli and La Videmanette. Soon it would gleam
over the Saanenland in perfect morning light, golden white
and leaden at once. My mother looked at the ground as she
walked, her shoulders hunched as though she could not
endure the mountains towering around us in all directions.
I held her arm gently to support her, despite the walker. We
continued beside each other in silence for a while, down the

uneven drive, and then I called for a taxi to please pick us up below at the intersection. It grew light. I smoked a cigarette, then another. Every so often I would glance back up to the chalet, to see whether someone might be following us over the meadow, hobbling like Jack Nicholson with his axe.

VIII.

We drove through the valley over to the small airstrip in Saanen while the sun rose over the mountains high above. It was the same taxi, the same driver who had driven us from Zurich to the commune the day before, as if he had been waiting for us. There was my elementary school, not the French-speaking one I had set on fire, but the cute little chalet of the John F. Kennedy School, below the late Gothic village church. At the edge of the airfield we got out, retrieved our luggage, and the car drove off once more. A dark green ribbon of shadow containing even darker firs still lurked beneath the increasing brightness around the mountain peaks, above which tarried, still a touch insistent, the clouds from the night just then fading. We stood there, and a single small aircraft was visible over on the runway, as though lost in the incipient morning sun.

"What now?" my mother asked.

"Now we wait."

"I hate waiting. Tell me another story," she said.

"I can't think of one at the moment."

"Please tell me another one, you do it so well."

"I don't feel like it right now."

"But if I ask nicely?"

"Do you know the story of the Schlumpf brothers?"

"No," she replied.

"So, the Schlumpf brothers, Hans and Fritz Schlumpf, they once owned a thriving textile factory in Basel. They employed thousands of workers, but at the same time had a major obsession with elegant antique automobiles, such as Bugatti and the like."

"And?"

"Do you want to hear the story or not?"

"Please, go on."

"At some point—by now they'd bought three hundred of these tremendously expensive automobiles and hidden them in a hangar in Basel . . ."

". . . the most expensive cars in the world?"

"Yes, Hispano-Suiza, Duesenberg, Aston Martin, cars like that. Anyway, at some point they'd put their entire fortune into this collection of automobiles, and then they found they couldn't pay their employees anymore."

"Makes sense."

"And the workers first went on strike, and then one day, one of them discovered, hidden behind a rolling metal shutter, the automobiles belonging to the Schlumpfs. And this was the reason they hadn't been paid, the whole hangar full of these treasures, gleaming chrome and everything. Where all the money they hadn't gotten had gone. And so, full of rage and disappointment, they took crowbars and smashed all the cars to pieces."

"Oh dear."

"Yes, and the Schlumpf brothers, who were inconsolable at the loss of their collection, moved into the Hotel Trois Rois in Basel, into a grand suite, and they sent for a *maître chocolatier*, the best in Switzerland, and instructed him to re-create all of the automobiles the workers had destroyed, in chocolate, in very small, tiny toy cars made of chocolate. The entire collection all over again. And when he was finished, they had him bring these little cars, and they arranged them in their hotel suite, and had the suite artificially cooled to a few degrees above freezing, and locked the doors from the outside."

"And how does the story end?"

"The Schlumpf brothers never visited their chocolate collection again, Mama. They would only occasionally peek inside through the keyhole, and at some point, they died. The suite still exists to this day. Its location in the hotel is kept a strict secret. Only the hotel manager of the Trois Rois knows where exactly the suite is, and he is prohibited from ever speaking of it. This was the legacy of Fritz and Hans Schlumpf. It was never to be revealed where their second automobile collection might be found, and it was to remain there, unseen and unadmired and unsullied until the end of days."

"Let's go to Basel," my mother said. "I need to see these

chocolate cars immediately. Do you perhaps know the hotel manager?"

"No. And you can't find the suite."

"We could say our name is Kracht. Like the ones from Hotel Baur au Lac. And you could just make something up, like that we want to see how other hotel dynasties do it. That's what your father always did, too, in grand Swiss hotels: sign the bills with the name Kracht extra large. Like this: K-R-A-C-H-T."

"You know about that?"

"Yes, of course, dear. Come on, I want to fly to Basel."

Sitting at a desk in a hut along the left flank of the runway sat an unremarkable man whom I asked to charter a plane to fly us to Basel. He was wearing one of those neon-colored tracksuits in Lycra, from which Speedos are also made, with a fleece jacket over it, likewise in neon, stripes on the side, and the front of his tracksuit read *Master Experience* or *Terminator X* or something.

Basel? Yes, that was quite doable, the man said, he just had to wake the pilot, they had a Cessna with a full tank, out there, one moment please. If madame and monsieur would have a seat, back there on the bench, it should not take long. And he lifted the receiver of an old green plastic telephone, waited until someone on the other end picked up, and whispered into it. Then he hung up.

The price for the flight to Basel, just a second, he had to

check the list, yes, there it was, Bern, Zurich, just one more moment, Geneva, Basel. He wetted his index finger on his tongue while leafing through the pages. There. Basel. That would come to nine thousand francs. The return flight would also need to be factored in.

My mother was rummaging in the plastic bag for the bills when a car pulled up in front of the hut with the pilot. The man made out a receipt, counted the money, and slipped it into his desk drawer. The pilot came inside and removed his jacket. He was wearing a tie and epaulets on the shoulders of his pilot's shirt. Something seemed off. And then the pilot and this airport character converged on us, and the pilot asked how much money we had in our bag.

"What bag?" my mother asked, clutching it tightly to her chest. "Surely you don't intend to rob an old woman?"

"Hand over the bag," said the pilot.

"No," said my mother.

"Thomas, take the bag."

"You've just said my name, you idiot," said the man in the tracksuit.

"Who cares?" the pilot replied.

"I do, because now they know my name."

"So what?"

"Christian, why don't you say something?" my mother asked. She shot me an anxious look, yet one also triumphant and vaguely crafty, and I wondered why. Once again my hand closed round the set of keys in my jacket pocket. Another inch toward my mother, and I would start swinging my fist, with the prongs of the house keys in it, right into each of their faces.

"Give it here," said the pilot.

"Okay," said my mother, passing the bag to the man.

He snatched at it greedily, crushed it between his hands, looked up in astonishment, and then plunged his hand inside, and of course the bag was empty.

At that moment, the taxi from before pulled up again. The driver got out; we saw him through the window lifting the walker we had forgotten out of the trunk and bringing it to the door. He entered.

"Madame, your . . . your walking aid. You left it in my car."

"Oh god, the walker. Thank you. And you, Monsieur Thomas, you will understand that we will not be flying with you under such circumstances," my mother said.

"I'm sorry, the flight is already paid for."

"Just give them their money back," said the pilot.

The man in the tracksuit opened his drawer resignedly, produced the nine thousand-franc bills, and slid them over the desk. "We're sorry, madame," he said, "We just wanted . . ."

"Rubbish. You wanted to rob us. You threatened us. They did, didn't they, Christian?"

"Yes."

My mother gathered the bills and returned them to the bag. The two men and the taxi driver exchanged glances. My mother and I exchanged glances. Everyone exchanged glances with everyone else as if it were an absurd Mexican standoff, up here in the Bernese Oberland.

"Are you still free?" my mother asked.

"Yes. Follow me," the driver replied, collecting the walker once more and proceeding ahead to his taxi.

"Adieu." I let the set of keys slip back into my pocket. My hand was trembling with adrenaline.

"Beat it," said the pilot.

"The Saanen airport is not what it once was," my mother said as we walked toward the car. "From here I would always fly to Hamburg with your father. And thank god the driver showed up; those bandits might have killed two people, but certainly not three."

"Mama."

"Yes?"

"Where did all the money go that was in the bag?"

We climbed into the backseat of the taxi and both exhaled. "Look here," she said, opening the front of her jacket. Wads of loose, jumbled cash were pressed against her belly. "And I'll need a new pouch soon. The excitement with those two scoundrels has upset my bowels."

We laughed out loud. It was the first time I'd heard my mother laugh in who knows how many years. And I myself had actually never laughed out loud.

"Where may I take you?"

"Please go to Basel, to the Hotel Trois Rois."

"Hold on, no, wait. I have a weird feeling our trip to Basel is ill fated," my mother said suddenly. "The business with the chocolate cars is perhaps not all that important to me after all. It occurs to me, though, I have never seen an edelweiss. In nature, I mean. Have you?"

"I haven't either."

"The edelweiss," she continued, "was formed from the tears shed by the ice maiden, high up there in the glaciers."

"Oh."

"Yes, and that's why it's time for me to see such a flower in real life. Let's go, up into the mountains, as high as we can get."

"With pleasure, madame. What is the best route to take there? Should we head toward Les Diablerets? To Col du Pillon? Then we can ask if edelweiss is growing up there? You could take the gondola to the top."

"To Col du Pillon, *avanti*," said my mother. "Pass me the vodka bottle, please."

. . . .

So we drove toward Feutersoey and Gsteig, toward the pass summit, which also marked the border to French-speaking Switzerland. The valley of the Saanenland bordered the Romandy on the south and west, and the archaic and dark-sounding Alemannic spoken where we were now yielded entirely to a modern Franco-Provençal just a few kilometers farther on. I cracked open my car window. My mother held the vodka bottle in her lap and sipped from it now and again.

All of a sudden, the autumn was full of wonder for me. I had always loved autumn. On both slopes of the valley, firs grew up the mountains in neat rows, small white clouds clung above, over the ridges, in them the promise of snow soon to come. And as I rolled down the window fully, it actually smelled like snow, too, and very faintly of rust.

"Why do you want to see an edelweiss so badly?"

"Because I don't have much longer to live."

"Don't say that."

"I know you've been quite angry with me for a number of years. Can't say my behavior has been perfect either. Toward you. But I am not yet ready to regret anything."

"That's okay."

"Never forget that *you* were the one who walked out on me."

"I'll try not to. Sometimes . . ."

"Yes?"

"Sometimes I feel like you aren't crazy at all."

"Ha! Me? No, that was always you, not me. *You're* crazy," she said.

"You think?"

"As a child you would always say you were made of glass, and could be shattered by the tiniest vibration. You didn't want to touch anything, bump into anything. You had this glass disease. I didn't know what to do, Christian. Later on I read a story by Cervantes, called 'The Student of Glass' or something like that."

"Cervantes?"

"In it someone has the exact same delusion you had."

"Fine, but unlike you, I was never in all those institutions."

"They weren't institutions, they were spas. Occasionally they were also just hotels."

"And why, then, were the front doors always locked, in these hotels?"

"Out of concern for guest safety."

"I no longer have the glass disease."

"You say that now. But any moment it could reappear."

Glass disease. What rubbish. I shut my eyes and rolled them behind my lids so my mother couldn't see me do it. Then we were driving through a tiny little village. I thought I recognized its road layout and proportions and even building arrangement, from my childhood. Planters of geraniums were still attached to the balconies of the wooden chalets everywhere, along with Swiss flags and the flags with the white crane upon a field of red, the crest of Saanen. I leaned forward to the driver.

"This is Feutersoey, isn't it?"

"Yes, it is."

"Would you please pull over here? There's this restaurant where we used to eat trout with my father."

"You mean the Rössli?" The driver stopped the car.

"Exactly, that's it. Come, Mama, we'll ask if we can have trout."

"At nine in the morning?"

"Please let's ask. We can see whether the trout taste better here or at Sihlmatt."

"I don't want to."

"Oh, come on, please."

"No, I don't want to."

"Why?"

"I'd rather not tell you."

"Does it have something to do with my father? Because the Rössli here reminds you of him?"

"No."

"He's been dead for ten years."

"No, that's not it." And she sheepishly added: "I haven't been inside a restaurant in who knows how many years. I've forgotten how it works."

. . . .

Oh, Mama. I didn't want to tolerate this feeling, for I knew it was pity I was supposed to feel, as though she were merely a poor child. It was the very feeling with which she manipulated people and ensnared them and squeezed them dry and then spat them out. But I still felt pity. I had never pitied her for her addiction to alcohol or her phenobarbital or her Nazis or her rape or her months-long coma under artificial respiration because she had always been nasty enough, but now, when she didn't dare enter a restaurant, I felt sympathy for her, a profound, swift, searing regret.

"You can manage. Just imagine you are an eccentric, slightly crazy old woman with a bit too much money."

"I am not crazy. You are crazy."

"Of course. I have the glass disease. Here, drink another big sip of vodka."

We got out; I supported her. Her upper arm was vanishingly slender, the bone palpable through her papery skin and the almost completely atrophied muscles underneath. Tables and chairs were set up outside. A waiter approached with a look of mild worry and irritation. It was a long while until midday, and my mother had already seated herself in a chair, from exhaustion, as it must appear to the waiter. He hesitantly considered whether he ought to shoo us away, but his Protestantism wouldn't allow him to do so, nor would his waiter's honor, and so he came up to us, as I had also taken a seat. My mother exhaled, heavily, and it smelled of vodka although vodka does not even have a smell.

"It has gotten somewhat more chic here, since the last time. Right?"

"No idea."

"May I help you, madame?" the waiter asked.

"We would like to try your famous trout," my mother said. "I last dined here forty-five years ago. You know, my son here, once, when he was still just a toddler, slipped his wallet into the pocket of someone else's jacket hanging on the coat stand here at your restaurant . . ."

". . . Mama."

". . . Well, anyway, there were crocodile tears, and since then we've always eaten trout at Sihlmatt in the canton of Zurich, and they were good, mind you, but not nearly as tasty as I recall yours being."

"We've changed ownership several times since then," the waiter said, visibly pleased. "But I assure you that our trout can compete with the best river fish in Switzerland. We've updated our menu, one moment, you'll see." And he went into the dining area and returned with two menus and silverware and a clay pot with thin Italian breadsticks he placed before us on the table.

"What are those supposed to be?" my mother asked.

"Those are grissini," the waiter replied.

"I detest grissini. Take them away this instant. And if you

bring me grissini again, I'll crash my Mercedes straight into your restaurant."

"Mama. Please."

"Yes, madame."

"And there's no need to bring us a menu. We want to eat trout, not this junk."

"Yes. Of course. We have trout au bleu with boiled potatoes and baked trout, also with boiled potatoes . . ."

The waiter had simply forgotten that it was much too early to have lunch. My mother had done it again. He disappeared into the restaurant, presumably to roust the cook—he was to fry up trout for a belated breakfast, there were two eccentric guests out there they had to serve, restaurant testers probably, celebrities certainly. A nobody would never behave like that in the Saanenland, the waiter had likely grumbled to the cook, because the old lady had also ordered a bottle of fendant du Valais, which she'd already drunk half of, after shouting that it had to be ice cold, glacially cold, please, or else she wouldn't accept it. And the man with her she'd said was her son did not look well at all, as if he were sick or terminally ill, and he took notes in a little journal. The waiter certainly was used to famous people and their extravagant demands at any time of day or night, yet they showed real class by ordering the cheapest cooking wine of all with their food, instead of aiming to buy distinction with expensive wine like the rabble. After all, he had enough experience with prominent visitors here in the valley, he had decades of experience with them, and it was written all over their two faces that he must cater to their wishes. Who knows all the people they might know? And the lady's mustard-colored suit! They had a plastic bag full of money, and a taxi was waiting for them beside the restaurant's garden. That they weren't carrying Louis Vuitton bags and hadn't pulled up in a Porsche Cayenne as C-list celebs would have done, but had the taxi wait, with meter running, was definitive proof. The cook had better quickly rub the sleep from his eyes and fetch the trout from the basin.

How did it even work, I thought, that the two had noticed I looked ill? What's more: who had told them, if not I? And how did it happen that the two had interpreted our amateurish performance at their restaurant as reverse snobbery? I had not even been present for their conversation. It was as if I had floated out of my brain and taken a walk, as ether, had flowed out of the plot I had been part of, even, and as if it had thereby become possible for me to be omnipresent, which, in the end, I was anyway, in my story.

Not a half hour later, and trout and boiled potatoes on white plates lay before us on the table, the fish like tautly constricted, pale blue corpses. Pinches of finely chopped parsley were strewn about. In the milky white of the cooked trout eye nothing was reflected. And what should have been? I didn't feel like eating, and so I broke up a potato with the edge of my fork and watched my mother studiously separate her fish from its bones. A small dish of cherries had also been served.

She had always enjoyed eating fish, especially the ones my father would bring back from his trips. It seemed my father was perpetually carrying fish upon his return, wrapped in oily newspaper. It was mostly smoked eel he would present her on the kitchen table at the chalet in Gstaad. The eel would always be sliced open down the length of its body, the skin shimmering black with fat, and the smell would be pungent, acrid, and smoldering, like a burnt-out campfire or a rubber tire in the sun, while the taste, for I was always allowed to try it, was at first very foreign to me, and it grew no more familiar to me over the years.

At the kitchen table, beneath the red-and-white-checkered drapes, my parents would quite nearly pounce on the oblong, tenebrous eel. There was something obscene about it, this disemboweling of the fish, the sucking away at the spine, the surgical removal, yes, the slurping of the dark, scaly skin. It was always a deeply private, intimate moment, as though there had been a tacit understanding between my father and mother to dissect the eel as the object of their lust, just so, and then wolf it down.

Fish had also been served at the armored villa of Franz Josef Strauss in Munich, my father would tell her later, after he had asked her to wait in the car while it rained, presumably out of fear she would get drunk at lunch. Matters were to be discussed, and the missteps of an intoxicated, no longer quite so young woman would have been unpleasant for everyone. What had my father told Strauss? That his wife preferred to wait outside in the car during lunch? And did he climb back into the car two and a half hours later and then say to her, thanks for waiting, and we had poached fish?

Later on, she told me she had a nice chat with the affable security guards meant to protect Strauss and his visitors from the Red Army Faction. They had smoked with my mother although she really did not smoke. A policeman had offered her a cigarette and given her a light. As if it hadn't bothered her at all that my father had been so ashamed of her that he hadn't taken her inside.

Franz Josef Strauss. The West German politicians of the day had always been disagreeable. Kohl, Genscher, Schröder, Lambsdorff—all of them had been riven, had been rotted and ruined by their appalling power, the exercise and preservation of which continued on epigenetically in their children. I saw the smoked eel on the kitchen table before me, unwrapped from its greasy packing paper, and I became nauseated.

"Who do you miss the most? Really painfully miss?" My mother shoved her fork with a morsel of trout into her mouth. I shuddered to watch her eat. A piece of parsley stuck to her front teeth.

"I don't know."

"Out with it. Your father?"

"I really don't know. Excuse me: you've got something there."

"Where?"

"Right there, on the front of your teeth. Here, use your napkin."

"Thank you. Well, who do you miss the most?"

"I think, uh, David Bowie."

"The musician."

"Yes. Bowie. When he died, I had a very hard time coping."

"I don't know him."

"But you've heard of him?"

"He also lived in Gstaad, just next door," she said. "I'd see him sometimes. In the winter he wore white Moon Boots. His wife looked just like him, if can you believe it; sometimes they'd even wear the same ski suit. They were both blond. And scrawny."

"I always really loved his teeth."

"I wasn't aware David Bowie had especially nice teeth," she said.

"Oh, he did, he did. They were angular and jagged and grown sort of crooked. Every time I'd see his teeth in a picture or in a film, I'd shudder with . . . with . . ."

". . . with what?"

"With love, maybe."

"Oh, Christian," my mother said, smiling.

"There was a film with him, *Merry Christmas, Mr. Lawrence*, a Japanese film, I think. I must have seen it at least ten times in the cinema when it came out. I was sixteen. And I simply could not explain to myself why David Bowie, who played a British soldier in a Japanese prisoner-of-war camp, would act so badly on purpose. I was ensnared by his genius."

"I don't understand."

"The Japanese officer who loves Bowie is played by Ryū-ichi Sakamoto—he's a Japanese musician—and he's also a terrible actor, I thought at the time. I was really embarrassed for both of them. I could hardly watch, even though I saw the film again and again."

"And today?"

"Today I think either the film was too small for Bowie, or maybe there is an incredible secret to be experienced in this movie."

"Oh?"

"Bowie has a spirit within him that is indestructible."

"As an actor or in his role?"

"In both at the same time, interestingly enough. And the film, despite being very good, could only surrender in the face of it."

"Sometimes I really don't understand you, Christian."

"I never understood Bowie either."

I sensed my mother wanted to change the subject. It no longer interested her. She took one of the cherries from the white dish and popped it in her mouth, stem and all.

Then you could see the tip of her tongue pressing against her cheeks from within, now on the one side, then again on the other. Her forehead creased into furrowed wrinkles for several moments, and then she removed the thing from her mouth and thrust it toward me over the white tablecloth. The cherry was still whole, while she had tied a knot in the stem with her tongue.

"*Voilà*."

"Bravo. I still know that trick from my earliest childhood."

"Did you know that we are being described right now in a book, like in Cervantes?" she asked.

"Don Quixote and Sancho Panza."

"Yes. But they are imaginary characters. We're real."

"How can we be both real and imaginary at the same time?"

"Stick out your hand."

"I'd rather not."

"Oh, don't be so skittish. Go ahead," she said. I held out my open hand. And she pricked me in the palm with her fork.

"Ouch."

"You see? You're real."

That reminded me, when I was a child, of the radio always saying there would be snow in Engadin or some such shift in weather. I had always understood there would be snow *in den Gardinen*, in the curtains, and suffered a blustery, seemingly never-ending, yellow feeling of vertigo, quite like back when I had begun building a one-to-one model of Switzerland out of Legos. And at what my mother had just said, I felt it again.

She carefully laid her knife and fork sideways across her plate such that their handles jutted over its right edge, and then she said we were going to drive to the glacier now, the trout was not as good as she had remembered, she would prefer going to Sihlmatt in Zurich, so we didn't need to ponder reality; it was scarcely bearable in any case.

I nodded and wiped my mouth clean by inserting my right index and middle fingers into the hollow of my napkin and swabbing my lips once or twice. She had polished off the cheap bottle of white wine on her own. I glanced over at her wristwatch; it was ten thirty. The sun shone. She placed a thousand-franc bill on the table and set an empty water glass on top so it wouldn't blow away. *Lazarus* was what David Bowie had called his last record. It had come out two days before his death.

IX.

From a distance now, we saw a gondola hovering in the air. It was a metal, altogether fragile-seeming rectangular box ascending the mountain, the upper half of which was glassed in all around, and which was then attached to a steel cable by means of a grip apparatus. Whenever this contraption approached one of the support towers rising up vertically from the rocks of the glacial massif, the cabin would slip forward and down for a brief moment, only to stabilize itself again with an intense swinging motion—so as to be reminded, it seemed, that it was not only traveling on an invariable route upward, but must also counteract gravity, which would have enjoyed smashing the cabin and its precious contents to bits against the mountain.

Up and up it went, into the ever-thinning air. On each side, the craggy rock faces sped back down into the valley below us, as though merely a trick of the light or of perspective. My mother had taken half an Ambien down in the valley station, and then the other half when the gondola began swinging with particular intensity. She asked me to hurry and tell her a story, very quickly please, because she was so terrified. She clung to my arm, I rummaged around in my memory, and what appeared to me first was a glass cockpit, and then the tale of Roald Dahl.

"As you know, Mama, Roald Dahl was trained as a fighter pilot, in Nairobi and Cairo."

"In the First or Second World War?"

"In the Second, of course."

"Yes, and then?"

"Well, he'd written down the coordinates for a rendez-vous in the Libyan desert, but not the correct ones, apparently, and so there he was, flying over the desert in his Gloster Gladiator, alone, with nothing to see except sand, sand, and more sand beneath him. It grew dark, and he was running out of gas . . ."

". . . fuel . . ."

"Yes, of course, fuel. At some point, the display needle thing was at zero, and he hadn't found the other planes, so he decided to make an emergency landing. He put down, rather hard, but a stupid rock was in his way, the landing gear snagged on it and sheared off, and his plane came to a halt, instantly catching fire."

"Oh no."

"Yes, and since he couldn't find the seat-belt release, he couldn't climb out of the burning aircraft and get himself to safety. He pulled and tugged and tore, and after interminable seconds in the fiery cabin, he remembered the pocketknife in his uniform, and he used it to cut the belt apart, crawled out of the cockpit, and fainted beside the airplane from pain. He saw the ammunition of his aircraft machine gun explode from the violent heat of the flames and the bullets strike the sand next to him, but after that: nothing."

"And what happened then?"

"He lay unconscious for a long time that night, next to the blazing wreckage of his plane. Since he hadn't shown up at the rendezvous point, his pilot friends had taken to the skies again to look for him. One of them spotted the flames in the desert below, landed, hopped out, and ran to him, dragged him farther away, gave him some water to drink, and Dahl woke up."

"Luckily."

"And his friend told him he looked horrible. He asked what do you mean, felt his face with his hands, and where his nose had been he found only a squishy clump of melted flesh."

"Roald Dahl had a fake nose?"

"Yes, they patched him back together at the military hospital in Cairo or Alexandria or wherever, but he always had a nasal prosthesis, later."

"Ha, yes, that's a good one. I didn't know that. He was a very handsome man. A fake nose is a bit like an artificial anus."

"Uh, if you say so."

"The stoma just isn't as visible to everyone, what do you think? As the nose is?"

. . . .

I nodded and smiled. At that moment, the gondola pulled into the refuge of the mountain station with a sudden jerk. It seemed as though several metal hooks engaged, anchoring the cabin within the reinforced concrete structure. My mother exhaled; her brow had become moist, in spite of the Ambien. I had not known she suffered from such a severe fear of heights, and I dabbed her forehead with a crumpled paper napkin I took from my pocket.

"Where did you put your walker?"

"It's being kept by the friendly man in the taxi, down in the valley parking lot. He also has our luggage, you know. Or did I leave the thing back at the restaurant? You'll just have to support me now. It's about time you supported me. You haven't done so in years."

We were led outside through an automatic sliding door onto a sun deck with wooden tables, an observation platform. Aside from three older Indian ladies sitting there pensively before three bottles of soda pop, it was empty. A deep ravine gaped to our right. The glacial panorama directly in front of us stretched southward for kilometers, all the way to the Dents du Midi, over in the canton of Valais. Only snow, ice, and rock were visible as far as the eye could see, an unreal wilderness in black and white, with a clear, sunny, enormous sky in purest sapphire above it, stretching up into the midnight blue of space.

. . . .

"So where are these edelweiss fields?" my mother asked. She put on her hideous Bulgari sunglasses. I really hated them.

The Indian tourists shot us a brief and inscrutable look, smiled, and then turned their attention back to their soft drinks and mobile phones. We took a seat on one of the wooden benches. The lack of oxygen up here went to my head. My mother reached into the plastic bag with the money and the bottle and took a large swig. A trace of vodka trickled from the edges of her mouth as she swallowed.

"The edelweiss fields? I have no idea."

"But why come up here to this horrid wasteland?"

"Maybe they sell edelweiss in the souvenir shop."

"But I want to see them in nature. You promised me they were here. I would never have traveled with you if I'd known I wouldn't get to see any edelweiss." She took another gulp of vodka. The Indian women looked up again briefly.

"I can't do anything about it, Mama. Perhaps there's edelweiss over on the other side of the glacier, down in Valais. You just can't get there from here."

"I can't believe it. You're not serious?"

"You know, I don't think we're going to see edelweiss up here."

"It's always the same thing," she said. "I could scream. I could really scream. My life has been an absolute pile of disappointments. Are you even aware how horrible my life has been? And you said we'd travel to Africa and I could see zebras one more time before I die, and I put that out of my mind when I'd realized it wasn't ever your intention to go to Africa with me. Only to spend my money on senseless, completely gratuitous experiences, without zebras or anything. And yet for years I've been hoping that my son, my dear son, would do something with me again, like that time twenty-five years ago when we went somewhere on the Eastern and Oriental Express. Where did we go then?"

"From Bangkok to Singapore."

"Yes, exactly. And then you only read your books in our compartment the whole time, too. If you'd at least have read something proper, Flaubert or Racine, or even Camus or God knows what else, but you just had to read your John le Carré, your trashy spy novels, instead of talking to me."

"Well, you were always drinking a lot on the train."

"Ha! I only did that because you paid no attention to me, those rubbish books of yours were apparently more important to you than talking to me. Plus you were always putting on makeup on the train. Can you believe that? Makeup. And now we're here at this godforsaken place, and there's nothing, no edelweiss, no zebras, no nothing, and you know what, Christian? That's just what it looks like inside me, too, in my soul. There's nothing. Nothing left. A blank white nothing."

"Yes. You're right."

"You know what this is? It's a sign of mental bankruptcy.

And it's a sign of *your* mental bankruptcy. I once read that in Daniel Kehlmann somewhere. The century wept blind. That captures it quite well, very precisely, in fact. This is my century, wept blind and empty and dead. You ought to write things like that, like Kehlmann. Now he's a good author. Not the sort of trivial nonsense you write that no one wants to read anyway."

"May *I* say something for a change?"

"This isn't about you at all. You always twist it so that it's only ever about you, because you're an egotistical monster. It's always just you, you, you. Such an unbelievable wimp. You shouldn't sit there like a shadow of yourself and always agree with everything; say what you think. Be a man for once, not such a baby."

"What I think? Nothing, really. Wait. Yes, I think I've been hearing the same sermon from you for thirty-five years."

"Oh sure, of course. Not to worry. Soon you'll only hear me in your memory anyway, because I'm moribund as it is. But you, you ought to follow the example of, uh . . . what's his name . . . of Knausgaard or of Houellebecq or Ransmayr or Sebald."

"Please. Sebald is dead."

"I mean follow the example of really good literature. Of books that last, not the sort of horrendous guff you write. Go and read Flaubert. You'd see how it's done. Learn from the masters. But monsieur wouldn't dream of it. Monsieur is conceited and obtuse, and then monsieur travels to some glacier with his mother in the hope it'll all work itself out. Preferably to the very glacier near the very chalet in which he was born, to conjure up some sort of catharsis."

"I . . ."

"You think I don't know what you expect from this journey? You said it yourself last night, in your sleep. Catharsis is what you said; there'd be an expurgation between us, you said, if only you remained on the move with me. Your mother. Takes her along to some saccharine melodrama, tragedy, comedy, whatever, starring yours truly. Promises her who knows what, seeing that she's got to drink herself to oblivion constantly and choke down pills for her unendurable pain. And then he blames everything on Switzerland, the Nazis, and the Second World War."

Boom. What could I have said to that? There was nothing, truly nothing. She was right about everything, in her delusion. She was right. I had been afraid of being unable to stop the juggernaut. I hadn't thought this through. Perhaps this trip had been too much given to chance; perhaps we shouldn't have simply traveled off somewhere, at random, perhaps I should've just booked us plane tickets to Africa outright, and we shouldn't have set out through Switzerland, just because, perhaps that really hadn't been very wise at all.

I told myself again and again that she was not well read, that she only pretended she was, that she hadn't ever read anything by Flaubert or Stendhal either—it was all just a bluff, but it was enacted so well that I fell for it over and over. Everyone had always fallen for it. She knew nothing of Houellebecq or Ransmayr; she only read *Bunte* and occasionally watched quiz shows on television. Even her subscription to the *Neue Zürcher Zeitung* was repeatedly canceled. She was an expert manipulator. That was her epic, incredible art, which I had known for decades; she lied and twisted things in such a way that everyone believed everything she said.

I had no idea what to say or think, except that my mother certainly needed a new colostomy bag soon. I looked around for a bathroom. There had to be one inside the mountain station. I touched her arm softly. Perhaps she was crying. I faced her. No tears. I turned back to the glacier before us. At that moment, we both saw, as did the Indian tourists, a small russet fox running about on the ice at some distance. It stopped, turned toward us and looked at us, looked directly into our eyes.

My mother asked quietly whether I saw it. All of a sudden, she was quite subdued. None of us moved in order not to scare off the fox. It was still staring at us. Its tail, with a white tuft at its tip, stood straight up as my mother whispered that it was hard to believe people would kill such an animal for its fur. I held my breath not to mention her sable furs scattered about various storehouses in Zurich. The fox turned away from us and continued trotting onward, across the glacier's sun-drenched, lucid-cold ice sheet, toward the south.

One of the Indian women took a pair of binoculars from

a rucksack and homed in on the disappearing fox, and I saw before me a scene in a Werner Herzog film about Antarctica where a king penguin walks off into the icy waste all alone, toward certain death by starvation. The penguin had left on a lonesome pilgrimage to the South Pole two thousand kilometers away, *solus rex*, and no one had the slightest clue why. The bird's departure had appeared like the beginning of its Dreaming, when a creature embarks upon a journey, incomprehensible to outsiders, not only to visit the spatial coordinates of its particular species, but to assure itself of its ancestors, whose spirits continue creating the world.

As was my mother's wont with her denunciations, half a minute later she'd already forgotten she'd spouted certain truths with such hyperbole that mostly you just wanted to kill yourself. Of course, it could've been the fox who made her see that her fit of nastiness was unbridled and inappropriate, but this wasn't very likely. In any case, she grew pensive once the fox had gone, and she closed her eyes. Her hand, almost atremble, moved toward the bag with the money and the vodka and the pills, and the glacial sun shone from above, unceasing and relentless, upon our little tableau vivant.

X.

In the course of this whole story, I must admit that I've never read anything by Guy Debord. A few days earlier I'd gone to that film event in Zurich because I'd wanted to act as though such a thing interested me, while in reality I'd only wanted to brag with intellectualism, like my father with his fortune. The big difference here was that my father actually had money, while I had not an iota of intellect. I put down *La Société du spectacle* after the first few lines, never read Hegel, and neither understood nor liked Lukács and the other Marxists. Still, I had realized, or been forced to, that the only way to deal with money sensibly was to give it away.

So I took some cash from the plastic bag. I took out a proper handful, and before my mother could say anything, or even noticed, I was standing in front of the three Indian ladies, asking whether I might join them for a moment. They nodded, gesturing for me to please take a seat, and then they asked whether I was Swiss, and perhaps knowledgeable about mountains. And I said, no, no, I wanted to give them this money here. It was perhaps sixty or eighty thousand francs. I began sorting and piling a stack of banknotes before their eyes which was not very thick, maybe only two centimeters or so, and then slid it across the table at them. The women were aghast. They all raised their hands, saying they wanted nothing to do with this, please. Under no circumstances whatsoever could they accept it, although one among them protested somewhat less forcefully than the others.

And suddenly, as these things sometimes happen, a rush of wind kicked up out of nowhere. A gust blew up out of the deep chasm to our right—you could absolutely see this wind—passing through the barrier railings and churning up powdery snow, scraps of paper, and, inexplicably, some oak leaves, too. A vortex hovered in the air, a little whirlwind, and then the gust swept over the table like an invisible hand, wiping, no, tearing the entire stack of money away. The colorful thousand-franc bills twirled about in the thin air and fluttered down into the abyss, just so. We all looked at the banknotes vanishing down into the rocky ravine, frozen solid. No one attempted to catch one.

"Christian. Let's go back down," said my mother.

"I am very sorry," said one of the women.

They looked very upset, like little children whose toys have been taken away. For some reason, one of them wiped her mouth several times with the back of her hand. I returned to my mother at the table, retrieved the plastic bag with the remaining money and the bottle and the pills, and helped her get up.

. . . .

"Peut-être que vous auriez dû le prendre," said my mother as she put on her sunglasses. The Indian women looked at her blankly. One of the women's shoulders twitched uncontrollably.

"She means to say you should maybe have accepted it before it all blew away."

"Yes. Such a shame. We are really very sorry, madam-ji," they replied.

It didn't matter, I thought. It's better this way. Clouds sprang up, and it grew colder.

"Come on, Mama."

The psychiatric clinic in Winterthur was an agglomeration of Brutalist buildings at the edge of a very gloomy forest. The interior walls were a yellow-lacquered concrete, while the doors to the stairwell and between the wards, which could only be opened with a buzzer, were made of glass reinforced with chicken wire. It was bleak there; it smelled of stale food and disinfectant. Men and women would sit there in chairs, mumbling to themselves and staring at the wall. Some would scream incessantly, whereas others were quite calm. My mother had been committed there involuntarily, one day before her eightieth birthday, when no hospital in the canton of Zurich would take her anymore. All of them had rejected her, my Madame Kracht. Winterthur was the only option left.

I repeated this to myself again and again, and especially now, as it always and with every new passing minute and hour seemed to me as though she were no longer mentally ill—maybe she had never been either. Perhaps the harrowing events of the past forty years, my forty years, that is, but also those of the forty years prior and the whole inexorable nuclear disaster of her life were, in her eyes, simply *normalcy*. Perhaps the misery, all that misery, had only been stirred up by me. No, perhaps I had caused it. My goodness, I thought, what was there left to talk about? The entire glacier, the whole world, and all the people in it.

What had it really been like being married to my father? What had it really been like living with her father? Had the SS identification card and the Golden Party Badge and the various torture chambers and the grandiose, decades-long, centuries-long silence, that corrosive, incisive, intransigent, irascible silence, been merely a dream, a seemingly never-ending, pedestrian, ghastly dream? I supported her elbow. She waved her hand sleepily; in her head, attitudes bowled back and forth as if the interior walls of her skull were the rails of a billiard table and the malicious thoughts inside just smooth, colored orbs of ivory, effulgent stone. *Elfenstein*.

Elfenstein. That is what the psychiatric clinic in Winterthur had been called. Klinik Elfenstein. It was a death clinic, I had thought at the time, she'd never come out of there again alive, she'd die there in Elfenstein. Never again would she see the snow-covered mountains or her colored-glass lamps with the dragonflies on them or page through her tabloids. Never again would she look upon the glistening flashes of the water in Lake Zurich, I'd thought, while the evening sun shone obliquely through the big glass windows and bleached the myriad colors of her cheap expressionists on the walls. Never again would she sit on her bottle-green silk sofas, feel the tickling fleece of the ivory lamb's wool dhurrie between her bare, rheumatic toes, never again would she forget to water the geraniums because she'd been too drunk that morning. Never again, I had thought, would the envelopes with bills from Ferragamo pile up unopened, never again would the presliced cheese in her refrigerator molder to the point of being inedible, never again would the Macedonian housekeeper slink through the flat with the feather duster in one hand and in the other the wadded-up hundred-franc notes stolen from her wallet.

My mother, submissive, would swallow the daily pills her caretakers in Elfenstein would give her with a little white plastic cup of tap water, not her own psychotropic drugs, the ones she had selected herself at home from her bathroom cabinet. She would never again go peddling Stendhal, or all her beloved Frenchmen, because there was no one there to impress with them. Her brusque thoughts, which she spun into malevolent sentences, would be but a single quiet meaningless voice among the cacophony of voices of all the other mentally ill people, among all the Napoleons, Stalins, and

Einsteins, hers would be merely a weak little old lady's voice, scarcely audible among the unbearably loud and dissonant tones of the men surrounding her in Elfenstein.

As a young, a very young child, she had fled west with her parents, from the Soviet army, out of Bleicheröde or Blankenfelde or Budwietschen or Bystrz. Her parents had owned an estate in the East, and then, *when the Russians came*, they packed their bags and took their place among the streams of people headed westward, toward Schleswig-Holstein, because the English were there and they, rumor went, would give the Germans *the most decent treatment*.

And what sort of decent treatment did you give the Jews? I would always scream, hiding myself upstairs in the attic guest room afterward to sob unrestrainedly into my pillow. And to the Russians, the Greeks, and the Danes? The question was always ignored within the safety of the thatched-roof house in Kampen, on Sylt, ignored unto the grave; only silence and humming ever issued from the wingback chair, and egg liqueur was sipped waiting for the daily news, and afterward the television was turned off and shrimp toast was eaten and postcards with pictures by Wilhelm Petersen or Fritz Baumgarten on the front were exchanged with the old *Kameraden*, and picture books on the Tibet expedition were inspected, and stamps were diligently collected with tip of the tongue wedged in the corner of the mouth, and steamed carefully off the envelopes using the hot iron and removed with tweezers so as not to damage the perforated edges.

At some point later on, I had discovered the music of David Bowie, by way of the album *The Rise and Fall of Ziggy Stardust and the Spiders from Mars*. It was the world furthest removed from Fritz Baumgarten. I knew every single track by heart. With the music from the cassette recorder and my mother's makeup on my face, I would photograph myself with the Polaroid camera, the cheeks of my childish face sucked in, my blond hair combed high with shaving foam. I envied Bowie for his crooked teeth and pondered for weeks how I could chip my teeth, or secretly displace them with a retainer fashioned from a wire hanger, so that mine would look like his. Once, I'd even tried to knock out one of my front teeth with a brick, but only the tip broke off, the lower quarter, and the dentist in Zweisimmen to whom my mother took me with some apprehension, the horrible Dr. Nacht, made everything whole once more.

"You're thinking about David Bowie again," she said.
"Where . . . how do you know that?"

I of course knew that she always knew everything, that she could read my mind. She had second sight; that had been clear to me since my earliest childhood. It just didn't often manifest as directly as it did now. She'd never bragged about it or used her gift to see herself in a better light; instead, it would always just seep out of her, as if she couldn't help it.

"I can see you better than you think," she said.

"All right. So what number am I thinking of now?" I imagined a four, medium sized and red.

"The number four."

"And what color is the four?"

"Red."

"One day you're going to tell me how you do this."

"I couldn't tell you even if I wanted to. I just see a red four."

"One more time, okay?"

"Be my guest."

"What am I thinking about now?"

"A playing card. No, a card game. And it's lying on a wooden table."

"Yes. That's exactly right. I can't believe it."

"You see?"

"And who else is in the room?"

"Your father."

I myself had not inherited this gift from her. I was merely able to find lost or misplaced items somewhat better than others.

"If you know everything, why then do you never know how the stories I tell you end?"

"How do you mean?"

"You're always asking how the stories turn out. Telling me to keep going with the stories. You must know what happens."

"It's too much for me to keep track of all the stories in the entire world and to know their endings in advance."

"But you could."

"Yes. But it would really be overwhelming. The space would be immense. Like in 'Funes el memorioso.' "

"By Borges."

"The very same."

"You know what that story is called in German? 'Relentless Memory.' "

"Very good. That I did not know. But that's why I have a son who can keep track of trivia for me."

We entered the metal cabin again, and once more she held tight to me. The Indian tourists remained on the terrace, sitting on the wooden benches, downcast. A strong wind whistled around the mountain station and stirred up snow. The automatic door slid shut, a voice over the loudspeaker issued buzzing instructions in German and French and Chinese, there were a few clicks and beeps, and then with a lurch we were headed rapidly downhill.

"Why are you so afraid of riding this gondola if you already know ahead of time that we're not going to crash?"

"I've been dreaming of these kinds of accidents for thirty years, almost every night," she replied. "The thing tears loose from the cable, plummets downward, and then careens down the whole mountain, three kilometers or more. The bodies aren't even recognizable as human anymore, so crushed are they. Train wrecks, plane crashes, my goodness. Give me another Ambien, please."

"It won't work that quickly. By the time it does, we'll be on the ground."

"Oh yes, Ambien does. You've got to chew them."

"That's not true."

"It is. They get into your bloodstream faster. They're absorbed through your gums." The icebound, jagged rock faces raced toward us beneath the gondola.

"You're not getting an Ambien right now."

"But I want one."

"Nope."

"You're just insane. That's *my* bag."

I held the plastic bag high above her head, out of her reach. My own audacity surprised me. She snatched at it feebly, a hunched, frail old woman with lacerations on her face who had to cling to the cabin walls in order not to fall down.

"Give it here. Right now."

"No."

. . . .

She withdrew visibly into herself. Monstrous rage lay in her gaze, but also a glimmering of fear. Her mouth drew down into a frown, her lower lip quivering.

"So how's this going to end? Don't you always know everything?" Hard to believe I was speaking like this to her.

"Please. Please. Don't be so cruel."

"No."

"I need those pills."

"No, you don't."

We were halfway to the bottom. Suddenly and without any warning, the cabin stopped. The vibrating drone of the steel cable abruptly went silent and was replaced by the howling of the wind. The cable car swayed back and forth. We hung in the air, fifty meters above the abyss, a fragile metal box on a silken thread.

"Oh no," she said. "I knew it."

"You knew nothing of the sort."

"Oh no, oh no, oh no. What do we do now?"

"What do you think we're supposed to do? Each take three Ambien and a big swig of vodka?"

"Stop attacking me. Take matters into your own hands instead. Be a man for once."

"If you'd brought more Ferragamo sweaters with you, we could unravel them now and spin a rope out of them. But you preferred to leave them at home in the wardrobe, in their original packaging."

"How dare you speak to me like that? Where does this anger even come from? If you could see yourself. Your face is totally contorted. All twisted and mangled."

She would soon regain the upper hand. So much for the stupid dharmachakra. I rolled my eyes, went over to the cabin's control panel, and examined it. There was a red button, a green one, and a black one. Next to these was a device with a kind of grille on it. I first pressed the green, then the black, which I assumed were intercom buttons. Nothing happened. No comforting voice spoke from the grating. The cabin continued to sway back and forth. It'd begun to rain; the water droplets streamed down the scratched plastic windows on the outside and then, pushed upward by the strong wind, back up the panes. I looked uphill, to the gondola station. No movement there. No one had appeared to check on us. The cable car operation was apparently fully automated. We kept silent for a while, both of us offended.

"When is it supposed to get dark?" she asked, waving her hands before her face. It was the gesture of an orator, a demagogue. "I just mean, there couldn't be anything worse than hanging here in the wind overnight."

"Leave me alone."

"Oh, these affectations again. Drags me up a glacier, *moi*, an eighty-year-old woman who can no longer walk properly and has to go in a pouch. And is now playing the grand seigneur."

"I don't care."

"Well, what you should care about is that I need a new pouch. Right now."

"Why didn't you go use the women's bathroom up in the mountain station?"

"Because, monsieur, because I can't change the pouch myself, damn it!" she shouted.

"Then you'll just have to learn."

"No."

"Yes."

"Don't be so callous. You're like your father, you know, just as cold and emotionless. You have his eyes. They were always frosty eyes, totally inhuman, ice blue, like an android. What you are is merciless, and ice cold."

"My eyes are green."

"That's irrelevant. You're not going to let your own mother meet her miserable end here, are you? I'm going to die soon."

"How do you mean?"

"Well, that's what the doctors always drummed into my head after the operations. The pouch absolutely *must* be changed. You can never forget to. Because if it gets too full, then it'll back up, and all that stuff flows back into the stomach, and you literally drown from the inside in your own excrement."

"Really?"

"Of course, my boy. You wouldn't wish that upon your mother, would you? And since I have such horrible fear of heights, you know, it feels like I've been having this fear-induced diarrhea the whole time. The pouch is full to the brim. And plus, we're stuck up here now in the gondola, without blankets for the night, without food and without drink. We still have half a bottle of vodka. But I mean, without water."

"I can get water for us by opening the window and holding this trash can out into the rain."

"Very good. Very good. You've begun thinking. That's it."

"Yesterday you were saying you never go anywhere without water."

"Did I say that? I don't recall."

"You did, when I told you the story about Mary Watson, who died of thirst on Howick Island with her baby."

"Your stories are always the best ever. If we get down from here in one piece, you must please tell me another one, all right?"

"Three."

"Okay, three," she smiled. "And now please help me with my pouch."

. . . .

I knelt before her, onto the cabin floor, and carefully lifted the front of her jacket from her belly. I undid the lowermost buttons of her blouse and found the beige thing, which was in fact very full. She looked off over my head, ashamed. Outside, the rain had turned to snow, the trickle of water against the gondola's walls had stopped, having yielded to quietly wafting snowflakes.

"There. Done. And now it's snowing. In the middle of early autumn."

"You know who they were?" she asked.

"Who?"

"The three women up there. On the observation deck."

"No. Did you know them?"

"They were the three witches from *Macbeth*."

"Oh, come on."

"They were! *Hover through the fog and filthy air!*"

"Why should they appear in our story?"

I went over to the window, opened it, and tossed the full pouch out into the driving snow. She tucked her blouse back in and looked at me. There was in her gaze something akin to gratitude.

"You should have asked the women that yourself," she said. "They would absolutely have told you."

"So why then didn't they conjure back the money that blew away?"

"Ugh, money. You think such powerful beings care about a few francs? Witches symbolize change. Their appearance doesn't bode well."

Such nonsense, all the time. It really caused me major distress. Always this half-baked knowledge, along with her certainty that if you only say it forcefully enough, no one would question it. And at the same time, she did possess second sight. My mother couldn't be disentangled, just as everything could no longer be disentangled.

"We need to make sure someone gets us out of here."
"Hand me the vodka bottle," she said.
"It's like we're going around in circles."

XI.

After about two hours, the thing had resumed its descent, just like that. There had been a brief, sudden burst of sirens, then a jolt, and my mother, over whose shoulders I had draped my brown scratchy wool sweater because she had begun shivering in spite of her quilted jacket, had said it would get going again now, and that is exactly what happened.

The cabin glided safely and quietly the rest of the distance into the valley. Down here it was now no longer snowing; the sun was out instead, and how it shone. It was certainly twenty degrees warmer than it had been a few minutes earlier. We got out of the gondola, emerging into a clement and pleasant autumnal landscape. Cows stood there, ruminating. The meadows blazed, green and saturated and serene as on a postcard. My mother wanted to complain loudly, but no explanation or apology was forthcoming from the staff; only one employee appeared, briefly, with a lopsided smile and a shrug, before disappearing again into his office.

"That's the Swiss for you," my mother sighed. "Almost Asian in their striving to avoid confrontation." She squinted in the sun, foraged in her handbag, and put on her sunglasses.

"Oh? Yes, perhaps you're right."

"No, I absolutely am. They avoid problems. Not because they don't want to lose face, but because they, the problems, are inconvenient to them."

"But we're Swiss, too."

"Who cares. The Swiss ignore complaints because other tourists will always keep coming. That's how it was in the nineteenth century, that's how it was in the twentieth century. That's how it will always be in Switzerland."

"Okay."

"Here is your scratchy hippie sweater back," she said, removing it from her shoulders with pointed fingers. "It's much too warm for me, and it stinks of sheep."

"I bought it in Zurich the day before yesterday. It reminded me of something."

"I don't understand how you can wear something so tasteless. You always used to look so civilized, in your Barbour jacket."

"Look, Mama, our taxi from this morning."

"Of course it's still there. I willed it to be."

"I wish I were like you."

"Well, you have been for a long time. *Tat tvam asi.*"

We walked slowly across the parking lot to the waiting vehicle; the driver had apparently fallen asleep. He had reclined the front seat a bit and was lying there with his mouth open and eyes shut, like a large, quiet insect. I knocked gently with my knuckles on the glass, and the man started up, as though he had been dreaming something peculiar, and opened his window.

"Nice you're still here." I opened the rear car door for my mother and helped her in.

"You were gone a long time. Did you find your edelweiss, madame?" the driver asked.

"Don't ask," my mother replied. "It was a complete disaster up there. First we ran into three witches, then we saw a fox, and in the end the cable car broke."

"I'm very sorry to hear that," he said.

"You needn't be sorry. I thought I was going to die up there in that metal coffin. It's all my son's fault. Come on, let's go now."

"And where may I take you?"

"To the German border."

"Mama."

"Yes, I want to go to Germany now. I've had enough of Switzerland. We're headed for Munich, please."

"Then we'll have to speak about the fare, though."

"Another thousand francs?"

"Well, I've been waiting on you now for four hours. More like four thousand."

"Agreed," said my mother.

"Five?"

"Oh fine. You did wait."

. . . .

I said nothing about this because it really was better if the money would vanish into thin air. But we were not going to go to Munich. Absolutely not. I told the driver to please take the autobahn toward Munich and winked very conspicuously at him in the rearview mirror, and he sent a friendly wink back. Maybe it really didn't matter to him that he was driving around two psychopaths; maybe he really only cared about the money.

"I don't actually want to go to Munich either. I want to go to Sylt. Onto a fishing boat, like Tolstoy. To be with honest people who still work with their hands and not with the internet or whatever," she said.

"Then why don't you donate your Ferragamo bags and Ferragamo sweaters to Syrians in the refugee camps. And your money, too."

"Yeah, I would like to do that. But do you know how cynical that would be? If the refugees wore my things? And anyway. How am I supposed to drive it all, and the money, down there? With my Mercedes? I don't have a license anymore."

"I can't believe I'm having this conversation with you. Who's to blame for the refugee crisis?"

"I don't know. Who? Assad? Saddam Hussein?"

"You're to blame. I'm to blame. Everyone who fills their car's gas tank and lives on Zurich's Gold Coast and drinks white wine and then goes shopping at Trois Pommes or Grieder. The people to blame for the entire misery of the world are you and me."

"Even if you only live off frozen fish squares?"

"Yes. Even then, I think."

"And what if you're too cheap even to buy those? If you only eat Kraft Singles?"

"Then too."

"And what if you hoard the cheese slices for so long that they spoil, and only eat them then?" She smiled.

"You're really acting like a child." And I also had to smile, whether I wanted to or not.

"Do you perhaps have a truck driver's license?" she asked the driver.

"Why, madame?"

"Well, maybe *you* might like to drive my clothes down to Syria? We would pay you very well."

"*You* would pay well. Not me. Please ... excuse my mother."

"*Pas de quoi.*"

"You see, he even speaks French! This is perfect. They also speak French in Syria, because of the Lebanon."

"Mama, they spoke French there in the sixties."

"You know what? You have a major narcissistic disorder."

"Me?"

"Yes, you."

"Should I get going now?" the driver asked.

"To the airport, please."

"Yes, exactly, the airport, but not to one with such pathetic crooks like this morning," she said. "And if we're not going to Munich, then it also can't cost five thousand francs, can it?"

"I'm very happy with four thousand," the driver replied.

"Then take the other route, please, the one onto the autobahn via Aigle and then maybe past Montreux. Okay with you, Mama?"

"Yes, just not back down toward Gstaad. I never, ever want to return to that horrible place."

"Deal."

"Very good, my son. It feels nice to make a definitive decision in life. I will never see Gstaad again in this world."

And so we set off once more, to the left around the switchbacks, down through the valleys of French-speaking Switzerland. It was a long way down until Lake Geneva first made itself known, as a deep depression in the earth can be felt before it is seen. For a while yet, the landscape seemed as in the Bernese Oberland, squat and in a circumspect way middling. Then the scenery gradually shifted, with the first vineyards appearing left and right, and cragginess and saturation began yielding to loveliness.

The weather was fantastic. My mother seemed to be in a good mood for the time being, and I had come to a decision. I would simply no longer react at all to her nastiness, so whenever she said something mean, I would just reply with something quite different, something nice and unrelated. In the same moment, however, it occurred to me that I'd had the very same intention just yesterday, and if I was being honest, in the weeks and months before as well. And if I were really being super honest, it had been my way of dealing with her for the last forty years. Perhaps, I thought, perhaps she really wasn't crazy at all, simply just malicious.

Shortly before the autobahn exit for Montreux, I remembered that she'd been down here in the Romandy before she'd married my father. And one of my favorite books came to mind, *Doctor Fischer of Geneva or the Bomb Party*. I'd always connected this Dr. Fischer, who lived in a large manor on Lake Geneva and would invite guests over to humiliate them, with my father, maybe a bit too casually.

"You were here as a young girl."

"I have no memory of that," she said.

"Yes, you were. You learned French here in Montreux. Long before I was born."

"I wouldn't have been here as a girl."

"As a young woman, then. Can you really not remember?"

"No."

"You were in a tearoom once, surely."

"Hardly. I don't drink tea."

"You can see into the future, though. How do you find it so difficult to look into the past?"

"I need some sort of reference point. Otherwise I'm blind to memory."

"Coordinates."

"Yes, exactly. Anecdotes, things like that. What was I doing here back then, according to you?"

"You were in Montreux at an etiquette school. A finishing school."

"And what did I learn there?"

"Well, for example, how to set a table properly, I assume. Knife to the right, fork on the left, napkin underneath. The water glass to the upper right, next to the wineglasses. The soup spoon beside the fish knife, the dessert spoon at the top of the plate."

"Yes, I recall. Christian. Those beautiful table settings. I would always do it like that at home in our Gstaad chalet and in Cap Ferrat, whenever we had guests. Which was as good as never, because your autistic, disturbed father couldn't stand guests."

"And you learned how to make conversation at table for sure. And arrange flowers. And perhaps even cook. Maybe that's where your aversion to fancy food comes from?"

"Hm. Maybe."

"Do you remember?"

"Now that you mention it, something *is* there. It's very faint."

"How do you eat asparagus?"

"You gracefully take the individual spear by the lower, thicker end with two fingers of the right hand and then lead the tip to your mouth by stabilizing the asparagus at the middle of the stalk with the fork in your left hand. Unless there are silver asparagus tongs placed to the left of the fork. Then you use those."

"Bravo. I'm so proud of you."

"You are?"

"Yes, really."

"I know! I've got it! I was at the Institut Villa Pierrefeu!"

"Here in Montreux."

"Yes. I took courses. Courses in posture where I had to balance a book on my head while walking. That was in the early sixties. Maybe 1962. At any rate, the year Bataille died. And we were given books to read. Racine. Molière. Bleak stuff."

"In French. So you did learn French there."

"I don't know French," she said mournfully.

"That's just not true."

"Yes, it is."

"What about your perfect quotations?"

"I don't know what they mean. I just toss them off whenever I suspect they might fit."

"No."

"Oh yes."

"You always seem as if you knew everything."

"That's just the posturing of an old woman."

. . . .

We both gazed out the window.

"Did you read Bataille?"

"Why?"

"Because you just mentioned him. His death year."

"Read *about* him, more like. Theories about how to squander money. Your sort of thing. If money isn't spent and given away senselessly, then it always ends up in war, invested in weapons of war."

"Well, that's not the sort of thing you read in *Bunte* magazine."

"No, of course not."

"So you read Bataille in Montreux in the early sixties and reflected on potlatch?"

"Well, why not?"

"Then you'd left the Nazi world of your parents miles behind you."

"Yes, exactly."

"So why didn't you ever confront them about it then? About how loathsome they were? And their insistence, until their dying day, that they were in the right? They were absolutely wrong. Your father was in the SS, for God's sake."

"You see in both of us how difficult it is, how impossible it is to confront your parents with the truth. And then to leave it all behind you in decency."

"And did you ever forgive them?"

"No," she replied.

"Christian," she said, leaning over to me. "I have an idea. Let's go to Geneva. It's not far. A branch of my bank is there. We'll pick up even more money, much more, stuff it in bags and suitcases, fly from Geneva to Africa, and give it away there."

"To whom though?"

"To the first people we run into there."

"I don't know."

"Oh, don't be such a bourgeois."

"*Me*, bourgeois?"

"Yes, you're petty and small. You've been trying very hard over the last few days to get rid of my money here in Switzerland. Don't think I haven't noticed. On the glacier and such. The money just fluttered down into the ravine. How much was it? Fifty thousand francs or so?

"More like eighty thousand."

"You see? And did I get upset about it? Did I say anything?"

"No. You did not."

"And before that you were wanting to give it to the witches."

"Yes, if you like. Yes."

"We are going to Geneva now and that's that. To get more money at the private bank."

"Okay. Fine. But I want to have a quick look beforehand in Morges, at my father's château. If that's okay with you."

"If we must."

"I'd very much like to."

"What's the point? More catharsisses? Do you say it like that? What's the plural of catharsis, actually? Catharses?"

"I don't know. Catharsis doesn't have a plural."

"No, no! Impossible! There's always more than one of everything."

"This is not what this is about. Please, Mama. I just want to see my father's house. I'm sorry that you were never there. I'm sorry that you both got divorced. I'm sorry that you didn't live in a château on Lake Geneva after the divorce, but in a small apartment on Lake Zurich."

"My, my! You really just can't let it go with our family."

So we left Montreux below and behind us and continued on the autobahn, skirting the lake, which all at once seemed very heavy and dark gray. Opaque clouds had appeared above Évian-les-Bains, over on the French side, and little raindrops now began to patter against the taxi's windshield, although the sun still shone here on the Swiss side. Grapevines were visible everywhere, and I realized my impression of French-speaking Switzerland had been shaped and colored exclusively by the few panels in Hergé's comic book *The Calculus Affair* that took place here on Lake Geneva. The vineyards sloping down to the shore gleamed in the sun and the gently falling rain, and I kept looking for a rainbow, but of course there was none.

I asked the driver to pull off at the exit for Morges, which for me had always sounded like a mixture of *manger*, *mort*, and mush. My mother had withdrawn into her corner of the backseat; she leaned her cheek against the window, looked out, and ignored me. I could imagine she really didn't want to see my father's house, that she shuddered even ten years after his death at the prospect of standing at his front gate. I, however, felt that I absolutely had to pay a visit to that beclouded place where he'd died.

Only the edifices of the ideas he'd erected remained; the homes themselves had been sold, rebuilt, and burned down. Gstaad, Kampen on Sylt, Cap Ferrat, Mayfair, the Esperanto of eurotrash. Those infinite interiors I traversed every night in waking dreams existed now only in memory, only as specter. The décor my father had so carefully cultivated his whole life—the sofas upholstered in gold silk, the Manchurian carpets, the shallow paper-lined drawers for each individual dress shirt, the Munchs and Noldes and Feiningers, the collection of Chinese porcelain tea jars—everything was now relegated to the imaginary: immaterial to be sure, but nevertheless real and eternally present, in relentless memory.

We pulled up before a large wrought-iron gate flanked by two old, overgrown columns with the obligatory enamel signs on them reading *Cave Canem* and *Privée*, and there was a cat sneaking off through the rain. I opened the car door and got out. My shoes got wet. My mother remained in the taxi and took a swig of vodka. I rang the bell.

What was I doing here? So many years had passed since I last stood at this gate, always feeling like a supplicant. Upon my departure, when I'd visited him, my father would always palm a thousand-franc bill into my hand. It had been too much to turn down and too little to do something sensible with. I'd always hated the money and taken it anyway. It was the same gesture with which he bought the favor of waiters and night porters. Maybe my father's Portuguese chauffeur still lived here; maybe he had been taken on by the new owners of the house. Maybe he'd been Filipino. His name no longer came to me. Perhaps it didn't matter either way. No one answered or opened the gate, and I did not ring a second time. My father's ghost was no longer there; the house was empty.

When I got back into the taxi, my mother said something, but I couldn't catch it. Inside, the car smelled of alcohol and of Ashes of Roses, a shocking wall of fragrance.

"What did you say?"

"Did you know that I ruptured your father's eardrum years ago, with a frying pan?"

"No."

"What do you think about that?"

"Did he deserve it?"

"You might say so."

"And what had he done?"

"Pfft. I hit him on the ear as hard as I could with the frying pan, from behind. He staggered toward the wall from the force of the impact and collapsed there. Blood ran out of his ear onto his dressing gown. He was deaf on one side for the rest of his life after that."

"Did *you* ever cheat on him?"

"We weren't yet married at the time, though."

"But you already knew him."

"Your father and I, we were engaged. I was twenty-four, living at Institut Villa Pierrefeu, arranging roses, dancing waltzes by day, and life stretched out before me like an inviting, infinite ocean. Such a wonderful time. I met a writer on a stroll who lived in Montreux in a hotel with his wife. He was out by himself and asked me if we might not like to drink tea together, at a café. He thought it might suit me, he said."

"You see? A tearoom."

"Stop it already with your tearooms."

"Sorry. Please continue."

The car had carefully merged back into the stolid Swiss traffic of the autobahn. It was now not just pouring down rain, but also becoming increasingly dark, and the windshield wipers could hardly keep up their elliptical work. Before us, on the road to Geneva, the taillights were mirrored in the puddles, orange-red and episodic, like little wet flames.

. . . .

"It was sixty-two. Yes, sixty-two. The writer had ice blue eyes, like your father. He was really very charming, and he made good conversation. His head was like a bird, no, like a magician. He wore a dark brown woolen suit; that I can still remember. And then I kissed him in an alleyway in the *vieille ville*, for minutes. I became quite dizzy, and when he left, I bit my lower lip. I can still taste the blood today."

"You've just made that up."

"No, no, it's true."

"I don't believe it."

"Why? Am I not allowed a love life outside your father's orbit?"

"No. I don't know. I can't imagine it. I don't want to imagine it."

"Because I'm old and unsightly now? And poo in a pouch?"

"Could we perhaps change the subject, please?"

"Why? You're always telling me stories, too, and I enjoy listening. And now I get too close to you for once, because you suddenly have to see me as a woman, not as some diffuse, ethereal mother-person, and you just shut down."

"Mama, please."

"No, no way! I am not the repository for your psycho-garbage! Just because you're crazy and you need someone to gleefully project your shitty ideas about epigenetics onto doesn't mean for a second that I'm no longer human, a person with feelings, wishes, and dreams, and yes, also with a sexuality."

"At eighty."

"Yes, even then. Or should I have instead walked into a lake with stones in my pockets in my late fifties? Just after you'd written *Faserland*?"

"This is not what this is about. You're just twisting everything around. I should be allowed as, as . . . uh, as an aesthete to not have to deal with my mother's libido."

"Oh, stop with these airs. You're simply not in your right mind. And you know what? Your iciness is surpassed only by your ignorance. Hard to believe, really, that you're my son. Better watch out that the glass disease doesn't come for you again."

"Oh yeah?"

"Absolutely."

"I . . ."

"You see? He's speechless, our Monsieur Huysmans."

No, I was not speechless. I simply preferred silence, as everyone had always chosen silence in my family, as everyone had preferred to swallow down and conceal and keep everything secret, for a whole dead, blind, and nasty century.

"And now?"

"Now we're off to Geneva," she replied.

"Excuse me," said the driver.

"Speak," said my mother.

"I was just thinking."

"By all means."

"Once you've left, I think I could write a book about this."

We looked at each other in the back. Under no circumstances could that be allowed to happen, of that we were both convinced. My mother immediately cast a magic field around us, a protective shield made of her psychic X-Men energy, so that no one could enter or write it down or otherwise get too close to us.

"That'd be really boring," she said. "Who'd be interested in that? A story where absolutely nothing happens, except that an old woman occasionally argues with her son."

"It was just sort of an idea," the taxi driver replied. "I can't write anyway. Maybe you'll write it, Monsieur uh . . . Monsieur . . ."

"Kehlmann."

"I already know you're not Daniel Kehlmann," the driver said. "Your name is Kracht. Like madame, your mother. I've been listening to you both now for almost twelve hours straight."

"Save for your nap earlier, in the gondola parking lot," my mother said, extending the protective shield somewhat further, the one with spines and the steel-spiked mace. "So don't exaggerate like that. And mind your own business. Pay attention to the road. It's getting more dangerous as it is. Especially for you."

"Five thousand?" asked the driver.

"Yes, yes, fine. Five thousand," my mother replied. At the same moment, we drove beneath the brightly illuminated autobahn sign for Genève Cointrin.

"You know what we're going to do now? Before we head to the airport?"

"I'm on tenterhooks," said my mother.

"But only if you also want to."

"I'm up for anything. Out with it."

"We're going to go to the Cimetière des Rois now to look for the grave of Borges."

"But it's almost dark already. We most certainly won't find it."

"Let's at least try."

"Doesn't your book *Faserland* also end like that?"

"Yes, but that was fictional. This here is real."

"Agreed."

"Please take us to the Cimetière des Rois. And please wait for us there briefly, and then it's off to the airport because we're flying to Africa."

"Gladly, monsieur."

"And after that you'll be rid of us."

"And I'll be five thousand francs richer."

"As for tip, though, sir, not a single centime," my mother said.

XII.

My mother and I poked around the cemetery after first having found the gate padlocked. It had stopped raining. The air wasn't really warm, but it wasn't cold either. Thunder rumbled in the distance, coming from Lake Geneva. She had her walker with her, and we searched halfheartedly, without much hope. The driver had lent us his flashlight, and the yellow glow sent our shadows skittering erratically back and forth between the trees, illuminating the paths and the dark, grass-covered spots in between. A little owl let out its enigmatic call, and we were about to give up and return to the car when suddenly the gravestone appeared directly before us on the left. It was fairly inconspicuous and almost overgrown by a boxwood.

"Oh. Christian. There he is," my mother whispered, steadying herself on the headstone. The walker had stayed behind on the gravel path, an abandoned black metal carcass. Her breathing was heavy and irregular. "Borges," she said.

"Yes."

"What does it say there on the front? Underneath the name?" she asked.

"Hold on. I'll use the flashlight. Can you see? *And ne forhtedon na*. What sort of language is that? Icelandic?"

"Old English," my mother said. I lit a cigarette and coughed.

"And what does it mean?"

"Don't be afraid," she replied.

We stood there for quite a while, at night, in the cemetery. She'd taken my hand. I thought of her death and of my own and what it might be like. She had almost been at that point so often already, in a coma, in the bardo, clinically dead, on a feeding tube. Perhaps it was only a very minimal, negligible step further, just a tiny wisp. The little owl screeched again. There was nothing at all to say.

"Well, and now we're going to fly to Africa together," she said.

"Come on, let's head back to the taxi."

"Keep your hand in mine. It feels nice."

"All right."

"Is that from *Beowulf*? The Old English inscription?"

"I assume so."

"Why did we not visit Nabokov's grave in Montreux? We could have done a tour of the graves of famous writers."

"I didn't know you were interested in Nabokov."

"Hm," she said. "Only marginally."

. . . .

We climbed into the backseat again, and the driver started the engine. I had always hated Geneva, that dreadful, phony, ice-cold Protestant city, full of poseurs and braggarts and bean counters. *Calvingrad* is what we'd always called Geneva. I preferred Zurich a hundred thousand times more.

"I have such a tremendous fear of flying in spite of it," she said.

"In spite of what?"

"The lovely inscription on Borges's gravestone."

"Then take an Ambien. Here, hang on."

"No, that's not enough for long-haul flights. I'm much too nervous for that."

"You could watch a film or read a book."

"Films? Me? Give me a phenobarbital instead."

"You really mean that?"

"Of course. I have a terrific tolerance for it. You know me. I'll take three."

She washed down the pills with a big mouthful of vodka. I wouldn't have given them to her had I not seen at the commune in Saanen how resistant she'd become now, after all these years. Luckily, she still had one of her kidneys. And three phenobarbital? That was practically nothing for her.

"*Grenouille, ciseaux, crayon*," she said. "I can remember it again, finally. It was the late sixties. I remember Gérard, our gardener, who would arrive every morning from Nice on his moped. And the completely inedible Russian salad at La Voile d'Or. Graham Greene came to our table and introduced himself. Do you remember? The zoo in Cap Ferrat, next to the king of Belgium. They had a really wonderful toucan there. You were always so afraid of the ape house because it smelled so awful. Our neighbor Somerset Maugham had just died. And my Dyane 6, that little rattletrap of a car. I'd an accident in it, around midday, on the curve to the Boulevard du Général de Gaulle. I'd been only a little drunk perhaps. You were sitting in the back and were thrown forward, and the ambulances came, and you cried and complained terribly of stomach pains, and then they took you by helicopter to the hospital in Nice. They suspected you had internal bleeding. I knew very well there was nothing wrong with you; you just wanted some attention. Poor little boy. I remember the moment exactly when your father showed me the Villa Roc Escarpé. He carried me over the threshold and smiled at me and kissed me and said, this is your home now."

"If ever you want to remember something from your life, you just have to say it out loud: *grenouille, ciseaux, crayon.*"

"Is it really that easy?"

"Yes."

"I am so very much looking forward to Africa," she said, and her hand slipped onto the seat. Her body slackened, and her pronunciation was now like cotton. "You made up for everything with that. What will we do first? I'm as excited as a child on Christmas morning. I want to see the zebras first."

"Where do you want to go when we're in Africa?"

"To the Ngorongoro crater. We'll have to take a plane to, what's it called again? You know it, Christian, you've been there before."

"Arusha."

"Yes, to Arusha. I . . . I'm going to close my eyes for just a moment. Wake me when we're at the plane. Arusha. I'm so happy."

We circled Geneva Airport a few more times until she had fallen fast asleep, and then I asked the driver to make for the autobahn headed north, toward Zurich. We drove through the night, and we stopped for gas somewhere. I sat next to my mother, sleeping deeply, and for a while looked into the darkness of the forests and at the electric green gas station lights. Other cars pulled up, people pumped gas, bought chocolate, got back into their cars, and drove away. Pale stars had appeared, and they shone like little white holes in the dark canopy of the sky.

The driver returned from the shop carrying two white paper cups of coffee, which we drank inside the car in silence. There really was not much to say. He went back for a second cup of coffee. I got out, walked a little way from the fuel pumps, and smoked a cigarette. We nodded at each other and both got back into the car. And then he slowly steered the taxi back out into the stream of traffic flowing northwest through Europe.

We arrived in Winterthur, and it was still dark. The city was awakening, cyclists were out, people were leaving the train station on the way to work. Our route took us a long while through the center of town and then through some wretched upper-middle-class residential areas, and I wondered what was ultimately worse, Brutalism or the nineties. We parked on the lot at Klinik Elfenstein and waited until it got light.

I fished into the plastic bag, gave the driver ten thousand francs, shook his hand, thanked him for saving us yesterday morning at the airfield in Saanen, and asked him please not to write anything down and not to turn it all into a book, which he swore to. Then I pinched my mother in the back of her hand and caressed her cheek. She opened her eyes, started a bit, wiped her mouth, and then stretched as well as she could.

"Hello. I thought you were going to wake me at the plane."

"I did. Don't you remember? We boarded in Geneva, and you slept through the entire flight to Africa."

"I hate it so much when I don't remember things. I hate aging."

"No matter, Mama, because we're here. In Africa."

"Wait, I do remember this car and this driver."

"No, this is the Land Rover we rented for the safari. And you couldn't know the driver either; he's from here."

"But wouldn't he have to be an African?" she whispered.

"This is Harry, a white Kenyan. Harry used to be a pilot. Well, he still is actually, when he's not busy driving the Land Rover."

"Really?"

"Yes. Last year he flew over the bush in his Cessna, on the lookout for poachers. He was tracking a herd of gnus over the Serengeti and flew a bit overconfidently, as people do here. He was flying barefoot. And he flew a curve that was a little too tight and lost control of his plane, which stalled, and he couldn't get it to pull up again, and the Cessna plummeted off to the side and ended up in a tree."

"Oh no, poor man."

"Yes, and the airplane immediately caught on fire . . ."

"Like with Roald Dahl."

"Very similar. At any rate, Harry was hanging upside down and dropped out of the plane and landed in a thorn-bush. He was severely injured. And there was no help in sight. So he first started crawling, and when he realized that wouldn't get him very far, he struggled to his feet, in pain, and hobbled in the general direction he'd seen a ranger station from above, ten kilometers away."

The taxi driver sat in silence, looking unwaveringly ahead. At the edge of the sky, over the treetops in the clinic's park, the first light of day broke. Dark gray at first, then, within

the briefest of times, it grew silvery white there, mixed with
an inkling of orange.

"So Harry here dragged himself eight kilometers away
to the bank of a river on the opposite side of which was
the ranger station, at some distance. His skin was hanging
in tatters, he had severe burns on his face and on his legs
and hands. And suddenly he saw that the river was teem-
ing with crocodiles. He found himself faced with a terrible
choice: die from his injuries here or swim across and find
a doctor."

"Good god. And what did he decide?"

"Well, you can see that he's sitting up front."

"Go on with the story."

"You don't know the end?"

"Yes, of course, but I would rather hear you tell it."

"He placed one foot carefully in the water, then waded
in. And swam across. And as if by some miracle, the crocodiles left him alone. Once on the other side, he dragged himself toward the station, then collapsed unconscious. Rangers
found him a short while later, and they flew him to Nairobi.
His open burn wounds had become infected from the filthy
river water, though, and there's no burn clinic in Nairobi. So
he was flown out to South Africa. And when he returned to
Kenya, more or less patched back together, he climbed right
back into his Cessna."

"What a story. And now he's here," she said, looking up front, full of pity and admiration.

"I'm all right now, madame," the driver said. I winked at him in the rearview mirror to please not speak.

"There are incredible stories in Africa," she said. "Look, the hills. And the light. It's all really extraordinary."

"The sun has already risen, there, behind the trees."

"There's a magical trembling in the air. Do you feel it?"

"Yes. Shall we go?"

"Would you . . . ," my mother began.

"Yes, of course. Whatever you want."

"Could you maybe brush my hair one more time, please? Who knows when I'll get around to washing it next, out here in the savannah."

"Yes. I'd be happy to do it."

When I was done, I clipped a barrette into her hair as always, and then my mother and I got out of the car. A Black doctor came toward us, wearing a white coat and smiling at us. She stopped, leaned her head to the side, and clasped her hands.

"Good morning," the doctor said.

"Morning. You're the huntress. Where's your rifle?"

"Welcome back, Mrs. Kracht," she replied. "It's good to see you again."

"Yes. I feel I've always been in Africa. It's like coming home. But don't you shoot any zebras on me. They're protected animals."

"We don't shoot at animals here, Mrs. Kracht." She smiled. "I'll go on ahead."

"I'm going to follow the hunter now. I want to go to the Olduvai Gorge. I want to go to the zebras," she said.

"I understand." I touched my nose. "This is only, uh, Elphinstone National Park, though."

"That's fine. I'm off now."

"You're going to march off into the savannah now, just like that, in your yellow suit?"

"Goodbye, my boy."

"It's easily two hundred kilometers from Elphinstone to Olduvai."

"I'll manage."

"Okay, Mama. It's good that you're sure about this."

"If we do meet again, why, we shall smile. If not, why then, this parting was well made." She put on her sunglasses. "Well?"

"I have no idea. But it's very fitting, as always."

"Shakespeare, *Julius Caesar.*"

"I'm going to miss you."

"You still have the plastic bag with the rest of the money," she said, gingerly climbing the stairs and looking back. "In the hotel, in Arusha. Or in the Land Rover. It's yours to keep."

"I hope you find someone out there who will change your pouch. And tell you stories."

"I hope so, too." She turned around to leave, but then she had another thought. "Christian?"

"Yes?"

"Thank you for all the times you brought me flowers."

I followed after her a bit. She moved a little way down the corridor with her walker, slow and undeterred. At some distance, she abandoned the thing and braced herself against the wall, her sunglasses still on her nose. It was quite hot, and the sun blazed inexorably in the African sky, although it was still early morning. She wiped her forehead with the sleeve of her suit, tottered farther, step by little step, and turned past the termite mound on the right.

"Wait! It was a really beautiful trip with you."

"No, I'm not going to wait anymore. I'm off to the zebras now."

"You are the stubbornest person I've ever seen."

"Me? No, that would be you."

"Mama! When are we going to see each other again?"

"Soon."